Year of the Unicorn

Year of the Unicorn

Carmelo Arnoldin

Life Rattle Press Toronto, Canada

Year of the Unicorn

by Carmelo Arnoldin

Published by Life Rattle Press, Toronto, Canada

Year of the unicorn /

Carmelo Arnoldin. -- First Canadian edition.

(New writers series, ISSN 1200-5266)

ISBN 978-1-987936-77-3

I. Title. II. Series: Life Rattle new writers series

Cover Images from *The Lady and the Unicorn* tapestry series.
Front: "Touch"   Back: "Sight"
Musée national du Moyen Âge (former Musée de Cluny), Paris.

Through Love all that is bitter will be sweet.
Through Love all that is copper will be gold.
Through Love all dregs will turn to purest wine.
Through Love all pain will turn to medicine.
Through Love the dead will all become alive.
Through Love the king will turn into a slave!

-Rumi

For those with the capacity to love

Prologue

THE STORY I AM ABOUT TO SHARE WITH YOU CONCERNS a chance encounter with a mysterious woman who held more power over me than art.

Art was my first love, a private world for me only, where I entered any time I wished and didn't have to share it with anyone.

As I got older and life did not unfold as I had expected, art continued to sustain me and give me a reason to live. The intense desire to create brought me great pleasure. Some people search for answers to the mysteries of the world in religion, in a god, in money. I searched for answers in art.

Still, I felt there was something missing in my life, an element in a composition that, if it could be incorporated, would turn my life into the work of art that it should be.

And then I met Farah.

One

IN EARLY MAY I WALKED ALONG RUE GEOFFROY-L'ASNIER in Le Marais, the oldest district of Paris, to the studio that I would call home for the next four months. The neighbourhood, with narrow streets and teetering apartment blocks, had a thriving gay and Jewish community. The area was close to many historical sites and a gathering place for tourists visiting the city from all over the world.

I placed my suitcases on the studio floor and looked around. The apartment was ideal for me. I walked over to the large window and peered out at red-tiled rooftops, cobblestone streets, the Seine river and, most beautiful of all, the spires of Notre-Dame. I heard the famous cathedral's bells sound through the streets like a gust of warm, welcoming wind. I counted twelve rings. It was noon.

I sighed and wished Farah was with me, holding my hand and enjoying the view together. I shuddered at the realization that without her nothing held importance in my life. Only with Farah did my life feel invested with meaning. She filled an empty void inside me.

I had never felt this way for another woman. Even though the circumstances seemed impossible, I had been powerless to resist this love, and instead ran towards it. But a nagging question stayed with me: Was this love a desire never to be fulfilled?

Would I end up in a trap of sorts? Was I on a fast track to disillusionment, sorrow and loss?

Nonetheless, no matter the possible consequences, I wanted Farah in my life.

"How strange!" I said out loud when I thought back to our first meeting.

If I had not stopped for a cup of coffee on my way home from an art gallery last spring, I never would have met her. I hadn't really wanted to stop at the Tim Hortons. I didn't really want a coffee. Yet it seemed like there was nothing I could have done to have stopped the car from pulling into the parking lot. The coffee shop shared an ugly, grey asphalt parking lot with a gas station overlooking the ugly, grey asphalt of the QEW highway.

I got out of my car, walked up to the plate glass window and peeked inside. The lineup stretched from the counter to the front door entrance. I turned to leave when I noticed a dark-haired woman standing at the end of the line. She wore a white blouse and green knee-length skirt over black tights. She tucked a stray black curl behind her ear and turned her head my way. Through the glass our eyes met. A bomb exploded in my head. I had a feeling of instant recognition. My mouth became dry. My heart started to beat fast. It felt like I knew this was meant to happen. She was the one.

I stood frozen to the spot at the window, then, seized with panic, thought I should turn and run as fast as I could, but instead I took a deep breath and rushed inside. All my senses were heightened. People chatted noisily at tables as they knocked back their cups of coffee. I stood in line behind the dark-haired woman and smelled percolating coffee along with the strong perfume of two women standing in front of her. A man and a woman in the lineup just ahead of them argued. The man wore a baseball cap and a white T-shirt that was too short for his big belly. "Eat me" was written in large red letters on the front. Grey jogging pants hung over his backside, low enough to show the crack between his butt cheeks. The woman wore tight jeans and a tight blouse with buttons that pinned her breasts. The man let out a loud burp. The dark-haired woman in front of me turned my way with an arched brow.

"It wasn't me," I said to her with a nervous laugh.

A second loud burp hit the air.

"Mike!" said the woman in the tight blouse to the man showing the crack of his ass. "Do you really have to?"

"What goes in must come out," he said.

"Yes, Mike, I know that, but do you have to do it so loud and in public?"

"Live with it."

"You're an idiot," said the woman.

Their bickering reminded me of what the old folks said when they came across a couple whose actions exemplified a less than common intelligence—the shovel has married the hoe.

In all honesty, I should have thanked them. If not for their stupidity, I never would have spoken to the dark-haired woman who glanced at the ceiling as if to say "I've seen it all now."

I smiled at her.

"It takes all kinds to make a world, even ignorant and uncouth idiots like those two in front of us," I said quietly.

She nodded and smiled back at me.

When it was her turn, the dark-haired woman ordered green tea. The smoothness of her voice made me hungry to hear more. I noticed a slight accent and wondered where she could be from. The clerk handed the woman her tea. My heart sunk as I watched her walk away. I looked back to the clerk and ordered a coffee.

I felt strangely empty at the thought she was gone. I turned my head and saw that she was sitting at a table near the front door drinking her tea. I paid for my coffee and walked in her direction, trying to muster the courage to approach her, longing for conversation with her—anything to hear that voice again and to be near this woman who held me in her thrall.

As I neared her I faltered and stopped at a table directly facing her. I sat down and cursed into my steaming cup of coffee for not having had the courage to ask if I could sit with her. I watched her out of the corner of my eye, trying not to make my interest too obvious. I worried she might catch me staring at her.

I stood up and reached for a newspaper left behind at a table beside me. I sat back down and held the paper high and pretended to read. Every now and then I would peek over the paper at her. I hoped it wasn't too obvious. I tried to determine her age, but found it impossible. Her face looked like that of one who would remain forever young. I was surprised to catch her looking at me over her cup of tea. She averted her eyes quickly to make it appear accidental. There was something vulnerable in her look. I drowned in her dark eyes, the most beautiful I had ever seen.

As I was pondering what to do next, she stood up, placed her cup in the garbage bin and started towards the door. I lay the newspaper down and gave her a slight wave of the hand as she passed by me. She smiled, acknowledged my gesture with a nod and continued out the door. I watched her climb into a light grey Honda and drive away. It felt like she was taking a piece of me away with her. A stabbing pain shot through my eyes.

For years I had built an imaginary wall that shielded me from every woman that crossed my path. Then a woman at a coffee shop, with only a quick glance, caused a sudden cataclysm in my being, the likes of which I had never experienced in my entire life. She held a power that made me think of Michelangelo's *The Creation of Adam* on the ceiling of the Sistine Chapel. As God brought Adam to life with the simple gesture of pointing his finger, this mysterious woman had brought me new life with a single glance. I did not expect the foundations holding up my life to collapse so completely.

On that Wednesday, April 2, at exactly noon, I fell in love.

I returned home and could not sleep that night. Visions of the dark-haired woman assailed me repeatedly. By morning I had made the decision to pursue her with all the means at my disposal. The fact that I knew nothing about her didn't matter. I would let fate decide.

～

As I sat alone in my Paris studio, gazing out the window at the spires of Notre-Dame, I recalled my last meeting with Farah before departing Canada for the City of Lights. I had begged her to join me, but she had firmly said, "No. I cannot go with you." She had smiled and then handed me a gift she had secreted away. "Do not open this until you arrive in France."

I looked at the suitcase sitting open on the floor. A small box, still neatly wrapped in bright red paper and tied with a white ribbon, sat amongst my folded clothing. I removed it with great care, and held it in my hand. Farah's gift was very light. I shook it. There was no sound.

I delicately unwrapped it because I wanted to save everything from Farah. I lifted the cover with shaky hands. A beautiful silk kerchief, wrapped around a lock of her hair tied in a red silk thread, lay at the bottom. I picked up the kerchief and the hair and brought them both to my nose. I could smell her sweetness.

I was touched by such a very personal gesture and ecstatic that a part of Farah had come with me and would remain with me for the duration of my stay in Paris. It brought to mind the Age of Chivalry and the practice of "Courtly Love" during the Middle Ages. Ladies, regardless of their marital status, could show their admiration and love for a knight by giving to him a token of their choosing to take with him on tournaments and into battles abroad. The knight would perform and battle not only for personal glory and the acquisition of riches but also for his Lady and for "Courtly Love." *Loving nobly* was considered to be an enriching and improving practice. The idea was rather contradictory for it connected sexual desire with chaste spiritual attainment—a love at once illicit and morally elevating, passionate and disciplined, humiliating and exalting, human and transcendent.

And Farah had given me a token of her love and admiration, just as the Ladies of the Middle Ages had done for their favoured knights.

I was a knight of the twenty-first century!

One thing seemed certain—she had given me a token lock of her hair because she wanted me to think of her, to remember her while we were apart, even if she had asked me not to write.

I placed the silk kerchief inside my left coat pocket, near to my heart, to hold me connected to her at all times and in all places. I vowed to take it with me wherever I travelled in Paris. I put the lock of hair back in the box and placed the box on a shelf where I would see it all the time.

Farah would be my first thought when I woke in the morning and my last thought when I went to sleep at night.

Two

I WOKE UP EARLY THE NEXT MORNING TO SUNSHINE streaming through the open window. I focused my eyes on flecks of dust floating in the sunrays. I got out of bed, walked to the window and opened it. The morning air washed over my face and felt refreshing. The leaves on the trees lining the roads and on the shores of the Seine were in full sprout. I had been told the morning air in Paris in early spring is often damp. Not on this morning. I looked out at all the beautiful churches and buildings that are so much a part of Paris history and was mesmerized. Boats, of many shapes and sizes, moved back and forth along the Seine, transporting visitors and goods from one end of the city to the other.

I turned around and took a good look at the studio apartment I had rented. It looked decent enough but showed clear signs of deterioration. I made my way to the kitchen and walked past the paint-stained wall that delineated the artist's work area. The kitchen was really nothing more than a hallway with a small fridge, corner sink and a hotplate that sat on a worn Formica countertop. Despite all this, it felt good to be in this small studio, in Paris, where I could make art every moment of the day and every hour of the night.

I ate breakfast and then took a walk. I wandered past many small cafes and wine, pastry and cheese shops that lined the streets. Taking Quai de Gesvres and Quai de la Mégisserie, I soon arrived at the Pont Neuf bridge from where I could see the Louvre. Despite having seen it on a previous visit, I still couldn't get over the enormity of the famous museum—a mountain of stone crowned by myriad windows laden with sculptures. Nor could I get over the line of tourists that snaked past the glass pyramid to the entrance of the Louvre. I elbowed my way through the line, to the Cour Napoléon, and looked up at the imposing Bernini statue of King Louis XIV that stood at the side of the pyramid. The king, according to historical records, was so dissatisfied with Bernini's original effort that the sculpture had been first exiled and then later modified by the French sculptor François Girardon to portray the Roman hero Marcus Curtius.

The horse is presented in mid-flight and yet in Bernini's original work, sculpted from one single block of marble, a massive rock formation under the horse's belly—a structural necessity to keep it from collapsing—had made the composition contradictory. Given the weight of the marble statue, what was an artist to do? The ways to solve such a difficult problem were limited. When Girardon reworked the sculpture to depict Marcus Curtius, he carved the rock formation under the horse's belly into the legendary flames which the Roman hero had leapt into—a clever way to camouflage the structural support.

Each artist had clearly employed a unique way to resolve the dilemma they faced. What route, I wondered, must I take to solve the torments in my relationship with Farah?

I had walked to the Louvre in the hope of seeing something that would inspire some idea for an art project. Deflected by the long line, I decided instead to visit an art supply store. I took the Number 1 metro to the Château de Vincennes station and got off at Place de la Nation, then crossed the square and turned on to Rue du Faubourg Saint-Antoine, made a right at Rue de Boulets, and entered an art supply store called Passage Clouté. I don't speak French and so I pointed and gestured at what I wanted— an assortment of paper and drawing materials. I wanted to be ready for the moment when an idea struck me.

As I was leaving I noticed a leather-bound sketchbook whose cover had the same colour as Farah's deep brown eyes. I picked it up and opened it. The pages of the sketchbook were of superior quality. The paper was good for both drawing and writing. It was expensive but well worth the price. I could draw and write of my experiences in Paris.

Perhaps one day I would share it with Farah.

I returned to the studio and placed my purchases—a T-square, pencils, eraser, ruler, various papers and the sketchbook—on a shelf by the work area. I stared at the arrangement, quite pleased with myself. All I needed now was a jolt of inspiration. Although the trip to the Louvre had not proved fruitful, I was confident a good idea would soon present itself.

I was ready.

Three

I SPENT THE NEXT SEVERAL DAYS PACING THE LENGTH of my Paris studio hoping an idea would strike. But my mind could only focus on one thing—Farah.

After that first time I saw her, I started going to the coffee shop whenever I could—always around that same time of day—and sat patiently at a table hoping she might show up. My thoughts would often jump forward and dream of the day she would be mine. On those days she did show up, I would hide my face behind a newspaper and observe and note her every move. She always came alone and sat at the same table if it was available. Tea was her drink of choice, based on the dangling tag at the side of her cup. She always read a book as she drank her tea. I would strain my neck to see the title but was always sitting too far away. It looked like a textbook because of the thickness. That led me to think she might be taking courses at a university or college.

One day I finally summoned up the courage to walk close enough to her table and saw she was reading *The Nature of Political Theory.* Just learning this tidbit of information about her made me happy. I also happily noticed that she did not wear a wedding band.

I spent the nights tossing and turning in my bed, wondering when I might next get a glance of her.

After several weeks it dawned on me that she only came to the coffee shop on Wednesdays. I often couldn't sleep at all on the night before a planned trip to the coffee shop and would arrive shaky from a sleepless night. With a surge of excitement coursing through my veins, I would check my watch continuously and worry whether or not she would show up. When her car pulled into the parking lot, I would take a deep breath and calm the tremble in my chest. I would sometimes lower my newspaper and let her see my face as she entered the coffee shop. I would acknowledge her presence with a nod if she looked my way. Sometimes when she was seated at her chosen table she would look at me, politely nod, and then continue reading. But more often than not she remained impassive, her gaze directed toward her book. I had to find a way to make her aware of my interest in her without scaring her away.

From the first moment I saw her I had imagined that the air I breathed smelled like her breath. There wasn't a single pleasing thing I came across that didn't bring her to mind. I studied her face and thought her so beautiful. I wondered what kind of man would not willingly scale every obstacle to look at her face. How could any man resist falling in love with her? Just a glimpse of her from afar brightened my day.

One Wednesday I remained in my car in the parking lot outside of the coffee shop. I had planned to follow Farah when she left to see where she went. I did not want her to see me stand up and leave at the same time she did, so I stayed out of sight, hidden inside my car. After waiting for a considerable period of time I began to worry she might not show up. But finally she arrived, nearly an hour later than usual. Through the windshield I watched her make her way into the Tim Hortons. A few minutes later, through the glass window, I saw her sit down at her usual table. For the next hour she sipped tea and read her book, and finally tucked the book into her bag and made her way to her car.

After she pulled out of the parking lot, I followed her car at a safe distance. She wound her way south on Mississauga Road. After stopping for a red light she made a left turn onto Lakeshore Road and then continued as Lakeshore Road became Lakeshore Boulevard. At Colonel Samuel Smith Park Drive she turned right into the Humber College parking lot. I parked a few spots away from her and watched her disappear into the main college building. I was happy in the knowledge she was studying.

I sat in my car and waited for her return. Students milled about on the grounds. Time didn't matter to me.

Although I had only briefly spoken to her once, I had become addicted to her like a junkie hooked on narcotics. I was unable to stay away from her even if it might cause me harm in the future. Never in my life had I followed a woman. I thought some people might think my behaviour predatory. But that didn't bother me because I knew that was the furthest thing from my mind. I saw it as a once-in-a-lifetime opportunity for true love. I needed to follow it through even if I was unsure of how I was supposed to do it. Nothing else mattered—not even my art.

An hour and a half later I saw her exit the building. I followed her car back along Lakeshore Boulevard to Mississauga. She turned onto Credit Heights Drive, drove past a few houses, and then slowed and turned into the driveway of a large house. I drove far enough past so as not to look suspicious and parked my car on the other side of the road where I had a good view of the house. I watched her take a key out of her purse, open the front door and disappear inside.

Then I drove away.

Four

IN THE DAYS AFTER I HAD FOLLOWED FARAH TO HER home I tried to work on drawings and a painting to keep myself busy. I had hoped doing so would make time pass more quickly, but I had difficulty focusing, and the week seemed to drag on. Wednesday morning finally arrived and my excitement at the prospect of seeing Farah made me so jittery I spilled my morning cup of coffee. When I arrived at the coffee shop I decided to order tea instead of my usual coffee. It made me feel closer to her and I do enjoy tea. As usual, I picked up a newspaper on the way to my table.

A few minutes past noon she entered. This time she was not alone but accompanied by a female friend. I discreetly observed her engage in conversation with the other woman. She was animated and showed grace in her gestures, her every movement unaffected by artifice, and she laughed with much pleasure.

Oh how I wished I was the cause of her joy.

I sat there with such longing that it unsettled me. It suddenly hit me how I had no control over how this began or how it would end, and being in my fifties, I wondered if it was not best to heed the advice of Cicero when he stated, "There are proper seasons in life. Nature has fashioned human life so that we enjoy certain things when we are young and others when we are older. Attempting to cling to youth after the appropriate time is useless.

If you fight nature you will lose. Fighting nature is as pointless as the battles of the giants against the gods."

But the fact remained that since I first saw her I thought of nothing else but Farah. I waited for each Wednesday to arrive with unbearable longing, and although I knew better, fight the gods was all I could do, and I was no giant.

I felt an intense loss as I watched Farah depart with her friend.

I then went home and waited again for the following Wednesday to come.

While shaving in the morning I took a good look at my face in the mirror. I hardly recognized the man that looked back at me. This was not the same Vittorio I had known all my life or even just a few weeks ago. This mysterious woman had changed me—I had become more open, more vulnerable, more willing to risk all.

I had never desired a woman the way I desired Farah. The only time another woman ever came close was back when I was a seventeen-year-old teenager. I had fallen in love with a beautiful girl named Hope. I soon learned she came from a dysfunctional family. Her father was an alcoholic who verbally and psychologically abused his wife as well as Hope and her two sisters. The father professed to be a good Christian and had named their girls Faith, Hope and Charity. I was never sure if he was being ironic or just cruel.

On my first date with Hope her father shook his index finger at me and said, "Make sure you have my daughter home by eleven thirty. No later!"

"Yes, sir!" I answered. "We're only going to the movies so there shouldn't be a problem having her home on time."

"You had better or else," he warned.

The veiled threat had me trembling on the inside.

"It'll be fine," Hope said when she saw my pale face outside. "It's just the booze talking as usual."

We saw *Splendour in the Grass*, a romantic drama that told the story of a teenage girl navigating her feelings of sexual repression, love and heartbreak. The movie brought tears to our eyes.

We arrived back at her home nice and early. As I walked her up the wooden stairs to the front entrance of her house, I saw that Hope's father stood at the top, drunkenly waving a long barbeque fork as if it were a deadly sword.

"You fucking *dago*," he screamed. "What did I tell you? Did I not tell you to bring my daughter home by eleven thirty?"

"But sir, it's only eleven, a half hour earlier than the time you specified," I responded.

"Do you take me for a fool?" he said.

He lunged down the stairs. His wife followed behind him, frantically grabbing the back of his shirt with one hand and fighting to get the fork out of his hand with the other.

Hope pulled her hand free from mine and turned me around on the stairs.

"Run!" she screamed. "He's so drunk I don't know what he might do."

I rushed back down the stairs pulling Hope with me. We stayed a distance away until her father, with the coaxing of his wife, finally staggered back up the stairs and into the house, still uttering threats and curse words.

"I'm so sorry," said Hope, her cheeks flushed.

"It's okay," I assured her and gave her a hug and a soft kiss. "I'll see you tomorrow."

"Okay. Good night."

From then on we decided we would meet at a street corner rather than at her house, away from the ever-watchful eye of her drunken father.

Hope was beautiful and she knew it. She enjoyed toying with not only me but also with other boys who could not resist paying her attention. She used the power she had to make us jealous and to make us do what she wanted. She made sure I was always on edge and guessing what her next move would be. Hope was unpredictable and her actions confused me to no end. Yet, in a strange way, it only made her more desirable.

Several weeks later, when Hope failed to show up for a date, I went to her house. I rang the bell and was relieved when her mother opened the door.

"Good evening, ma'am," I said. "I-I'm sorry to disturb you. Is Hope home?"

"No," she answered. "She went out with her older sister."

"Where to?"

"I don't know."

I checked the usual haunts and didn't find her. I decided to chance the Olympic Dance Hall, which was known for being wild. I knew that boys got to drinking and fighting at the hall just for the sake of "proving" they were men. I found it all rather stupid.

When I arrived, a group of teenage boys stood at the door, with greased ducktail haircuts and packs of cigarettes tucked in the rolled-up sleeves of their T-shirts. They had a bottle of liquor hidden in a brown paper bag they shared between drags of a cigarette, and kept a watchful eye for the police who regularly came around. They gave me the once over but stepped aside and let me enter. The hall was big and dark. The place was packed. People were swinging on the dance floor. Coloured lights danced along the walls and ceiling. The energy electrified me. My heart thumped with the loud beat of the drums as I pushed between the dancers and onlookers.

I heard a sudden burst of clapping and screams of "yes, yes, yes" above the music. At the back of the dance floor, a group of teenagers clapped their hands and screamed "the more we clap the more comes off, the more we clap the more comes off." I inched my way to the back.

Hope and her sister Faith were dancing on a table, showing their naked breasts under the flashing lights. I watched some boys reach out to try and touch them. The girls swivelled their hips back and forth to the music and strategically avoided the reaching hands. It was obvious by the excitement on the sisters' faces that they enjoyed the crowd's attention and the moment of danger it provided. I stood still as a statue.

The shock of seeing Hope this way hit me so hard I had to fight to get my breath back. I needed fresh air. I pushed my way through the crowd and out the door. I was so upset I walked all the way home in a daze. I came to the realization that I had to let Hope go. I spent many nights moping about our doomed relationship and wishing things could have been different. For weeks I had no appetite and lost weight. I dared to curse God for placing me in such a predicament. I even had thoughts of killing myself.

Then something miraculous happened. The turmoil pushed me towards what would become my true love—art. Suffering can ignite artistic creativity, which happiness has a tendency to stem. I channelled my anguish by travelling along the craggy shores of Nova Scotia to paint pictures of an angry sea. To my surprise I later discovered the great English artist J.M.W. Turner had done the same in his younger days.

More than thirty years had passed since then, and I never again fully trusted any women who came into my life. I would not allow myself to be open and vulnerable. Never again was I going to get hurt.

Farah changed everything. I didn't want to be careful anymore. I wanted to let myself go into free fall.

Five

MY MIND RARELY STRAYED FAR FROM FARAH AND WHAT she might be doing—I waited and lived only to catch a glimpse of her on Wednesdays—and it hindered the artistic inspiration I sought for my artwork. The longing brought on by her absence overshadowed everything. I lived in a Toronto studio located in an industrial building on Carlaw Avenue between Dundas and Queen Street East. The apartment had been my residence for most of my adult life, since arriving in Toronto. It had become the central place in my life where I could avoid the outside world, and then reinvent the world in a way that best suited my ideas, needs and personality.

The studio was spacious with large windows on the north and west side that allowed generous amounts of natural light. For some time I had been working on a large painting that grappled with society's alienation at the hands of governments and multinational corporations. But I had been unable to concentrate since I first saw Farah. Her face swirled around in my head and made it impossible for me to paint.

Bach's "Magnificat," Handel's "Coronation Anthems," Beethoven's piano sonatas and Richard Strauss's "Der Rosenkavalier" usually had the power to create the atmosphere I needed to work. I played them over and over to get my mind off Farah.

That failed.

I turned to a new work hoping it might do the trick. I planned a piece suggesting a strange narrative that presented the viewer with the enigma of disparate elements cobbled together and placed side by side to depict a struggle. I wanted the painting to have a social conscience and to entice the viewer to question what takes place in the world around them, reflecting the good and bad of contemporary life.

That failed.

I started another painting with mountains and other landscape vignettes in saturated colours, intertwined with snippets of architecture and people from past eras—nothing made clear as to what they're doing or the reason they're doing it. I wanted to make the image as challenging as the times we lived in. I wanted my work to bring about change in society and not ignore the real problems that most people face on a daily basis.

The mountain needed a sharper green, I thought—then I saw Farah's face.

On impulse I decided to drive to her house.

The morning sky was filled with dark grey clouds and cold rain splattered the windshield of my car as I drove to Farah's home. Her car was parked in the driveway. I decided the bad weather would provide good cover as I parked my car far enough away that if she happened to look out the window she wouldn't see me. I sat in the car for a few minutes and staked out her house through the rearview mirror. Rivulets of water ran down the rear windshield. I grabbed my umbrella from the back seat and opened the door. I slowly walked up the street, my umbrella angled down and forward to avoid the downpour, and to cover my face. A strong wind blew the rain in all directions. By the time I got to her house my coat and clothes were soaked. I lightly treaded halfway up the front yard, along a shelter of tall bushes. I peeked through the branches to the windows in the hope of seeing her shadow cross a room behind the sheer curtains.

A wet coldness worked itself into my bones. After what seemed like an eternity, I shivered my way back to the car.

Back inside my warm studio apartment I stood in my sopping wet clothes. A puddle formed around my feet. I felt hopelessly alone. After changing into dry clothes, I stood in front of the painting I had walked away from. For a brief moment I considered returning to it but instead I recalled the first time I had followed Farah home. I thought of my countless visits to Tim Hortons to watch her from a distance and of how, in all that time, I had not attempted to speak with her, not since our first chance meeting.

The disappointment of the morning rolled over me.

I vowed that no matter what the next time I saw Farah I would approach her.

What did I have to lose?

Six

THE FOLLOWING WEDNESDAY I DROVE TO THE COFFEE shop a little earlier than usual. I took my coffee to the table where I normally sat and waited for Farah to arrive. She entered shortly after noon and headed straight for her usual table where she deposited her thick book. I observed her every move. She joined the lineup, smiling at people along the way, ordered a tea and then returned to her table with it.

I tried to sneak a look at those dark eyes and the beguiling gaze that haunted my dreams. Their mystery drew me to her as water draws the light of the sun. From my table and over my newspaper I could clearly see her perfectly arched eyebrows above her open book. They were dark like her hair. She had a high forehead and classical nose. Her skin was blemish-free and possessed a creaminess that, against the darkness of her hair, exuded a mother of pearl shine. Her most intoxicating feature was her warm and contagious smile.

"She is truly beautiful," I said under my breath.

I was nervous but determined to talk to her. As I was building up the courage to approach her, a dishevelled teenager entered the coffee shop. He appeared confused, as if he had entered the wrong place, or was perhaps looking for a specific person that he could not see. He walked to the counter and ordered a coffee. Instead of finding a table to sit at, he stood by the counter, sipping his coffee, and stared in the direction of Farah. Perhaps, like me, he simply found her attractive.

His focus shifted to Farah's purse sitting on the chair next to her. He rushed towards it. I jerked to the edge of my seat, ready to dash to her rescue. Farah reached into her purse at almost the same time he reached her table, and without taking her eyes away from her open book she pulled out a tissue. When the teenager saw the purse in her hands, he continued past her table and out the door. Farah had been so engrossed in her book she hadn't noticed the near-miss theft. Part of me was sorry he had failed because it would have given me a reason to act and the opportunity to be her hero—or at least it would have given me an excuse to talk to her.

I sat with my heart pounding and was about to stand and approach her when she thumped her book closed on the table. She stood up, gathered her jacket and purse and began walking towards the door.

I was so disappointed in myself. I should have approached her earlier, before even the boy had arrived. It made my stomach churn. I sat feeling sorry for myself for blowing it again when I noticed that her book still sat on the table. I rushed over and picked it up and ran after her to the parking lot.

She was standing by the side of her car, brow furrowed, fumbling through her purse. She shook her head as if she realized she'd forgotten something and turned back toward the entrance of the shop. She met my gaze.

"Excuse me," I said and swallowed hard. "You forgot your book."

"Oh."

She spoke so casually, as if standing directly in front of me didn't make her knees go weak, as mine did in front of her.

"Thank you so very much," she said. "I have no idea where my mind is sometimes. God only knows when I'm mentally tired I can't function, as you can obviously see."

"There's nothing to be ashamed about," I responded. "We all forget things occasionally."

She searched through her purse one more time in a hurried manner and accidentally knocked something to the ground.

"Let me get that," I said and bent over.

We both knelt down at the same time and our hands touched as we both reached for the fallen hairbrush.

"Excuse me," I said.

Farah's gaze locked on mine long enough for me to feel a rush of heat on my face. Her cheeks turned pink.

I handed her the hairbrush.

"Thanks," she said and went back to rummaging through her purse.

"Oh no!" she cried out when she peered inside the driver's window and slapped the roof of the car. "No, no, no! How stupid can I be?"

"What's wrong?" I asked.

"I am so inept today I locked my keys inside the car and I don't have a spare set with me."

"Don't be so upset with yourself," I said. "I've done the same thing."

"What am I going to do now?"

"I think I might be able to help."

"How?"

"Wait here."

I once saw a man outside a bookshop on Bloor Street using a coat hanger to open the door of his car.

"I'll be right back," I told her.

I rushed back inside the coffee shop and explained the situation to the manager. He handed me a knife and a wire coat hanger. I made my way back to the car. I unravelled and bent the coat hanger and then gently pressed the glass away from the window's insulating strip. I carefully pried the glass with the knife and pressed downwards. I lifted the glass a bit more so that I could slip the coat hanger inside and drop it down far enough to catch on the lock button. I made a few attempts and then heard a *click*.

"Oh my God, you did it!" she cried out. "Thank you so much. I don't know how to thank you."

"Oh, please," I said. "I'm happy to do it."

"How about I treat you to tea or coffee?"

"That would be nice," I said.

Her smile warmed my skin in a way the sun never could.

As I held the door open for Farah, I couldn't believe my luck. I was about to have tea with the woman of my dreams. Yet facing the simple task of having a conversation with her paralyzed me with fear. I had no way of understanding the sudden and powerful attraction I felt toward this woman who I knew nothing about. I had never experienced these feelings with any other women I had known in my life.

Being near her transported me to an ideal and imaginary world filled with happiness. The enchantment she provided rendered all other needs I had meaningless and irrelevant. I had to hold onto this love with both hands.

Farah had arrived in my life like a flash that illuminated the possibility of a happiness that I had never known. It now seemed unbearably lonely to just let the safe things in life drive me from one moment to the next. I would not allow my fear to turn this into a situation like that of Dante and Beatrice, with Dante pining for years at the sight of Beatrice, who besotted him, but who he never spoke to in his entire life.

We entered the shop and at the counter I turned to Farah and said, "What will it be?"

"Oh, no," she said putting her hand up as if to stop me from moving. "Please let me treat you."

"Please. I insist. It would be my pleasure to get you something."

She stood there a moment, quietly, as if not knowing how to proceed, and finally smiled. "Green tea, please," she said.

I ordered her tea and coffee for myself and then I followed her to her table and sat down across from her. "It's awfully busy here today," I said to get the conversation started.

"From what I have observed in the past, it seems to be like that most of the times I come here."

"I hope after the trouble you have just gone through you are relaxed enough to enjoy your tea."

She smiled at me and said, "Thanks to you, I am now relaxed and I will do my best to enjoy the tea."

Our easy exchange of words had given me hope and after a few moments I stopped and said, "I'm sorry. We've been talking for a while and I haven't introduced myself." I was nervous and felt like a little boy. "M-m-my name is Vittorio Lampi."

She smiled and accepted my hand.

"I'm Farah Pavani," she said with a smile and shook my hand. "I'm pleased to meet you, Vittorio Lampi."

After a moment of silence I finally said, "I don't know if you remember me, but we met briefly weeks ago, here, in the lineup."

She pointed a perfectly manicured finger at me. "Yes, come to think of it, I have noticed you on occasion here."

"I was here on a Wednesday," I said. "You may recall the burping idiot in the lineup ahead of us, the very first time we met?"

"Ha," she said. "I remember him."

"That wasn't the most auspicious way of meeting anyone, but better than not meeting you at all," I said.

Farah's face flushed at my remark and her eyes lit up. "I'm glad we met, too," she said.

Hearing the word "glad" filled me with hope.

"If you don't mind me saying so, you look like you could be Sicilian," I said. "I detect a slight accent. Where are you from?"

"I'm *Canadian*," she said in a definite manner that made it clear she did not want to pursue this line of questioning.

"I'm Italian in origin," I said. "*Vittorio*, my first name, means 'victorious,' and my last name, *Lampi*, means 'bolt of lightning.' You could say that I'm a victorious bolt of lightning. So if you come close to me you had better watch out."

I laughed and so did she.

"Very funny," she said. "The quick way in which you fixed my car problem is surely a testament to your last name."

"To be honest, I didn't know I had it in me."

"Since you're interested in the meaning of names, Farah means *joy*," she said.

"Well it's certainly a joy talking to you."

"Please." She looked straight at me. "There is no need for flattery."

"I noticed you're reading a textbook," I said, changing the subject. "Are you taking a course?"

"Yes, at Humber College."

I looked down at her book. "Political Science?"

"Yes," she said, "and also philosophy."

"That's great—good philosophers are the conscience of society. What do you dream to do when you're done with your education? A politician? A philosopher?"

"In the end one never knows what will determine what one will do. Some things I believe are predetermined."

"You have a point there," I said. "Fate has a way of arranging things we don't foresee."

"In life that's often the case, "Farah said and then took a sip of her tea.

"I'm an artist," I said.

"An artist? I also have an interest in art."

"Really?"

She glanced out the window, looking in deep thought about something, and then checked her watch. I was worried she found our conversation boring and wished I could think of something to say that would capture her attention again.

"Oh, dear," she said. Her forehead creased with worry. "I'm sorry. I have to go."

"Sorry to hear that," I said.

She stood up and extended her hand.

"Thank you again for both retrieving my book and for your kindness in assisting me with my car problem," she said.

"Oh, it was nothing."

"Nonetheless, thank you so much."

"Well then, until next Wednesday?" I said.

"Next Wednesday?"

"Yes, for coffee or tea?"

"One never knows," she replied as if she couldn't promise anything.

"Not that I would mind, but for your own well-being, I hope I will not be required to do another rescue in order to have tea with you," I joked.

"Hopefully not," she said and smiled.

At the door she turned back and gave me a wave of her hand.

Seven

I SAT IN MY TORONTO STUDIO APARTMENT STARING AT the painting I was working on. I could not decide how it was coming along and worried that once I was finished and had a bit of distance from it, the work would not turn out as good as I had imagined. No painting ever completely lived up to my intentions or expectations. But nothing was worse than those times when art utterly refused to cooperate and mercilessly kicked one in the gut. I was hoping this new painting would not turn out to be one of those occasions.

I also worried about my finances as I contemplated the work. Becoming a successful artist was as likely as winning a million dollars in a lottery. Aspiring artists like me were more often than not ignored by the so-called art experts and only taken seriously when validated by someone from the elite. The daunting task of choosing what art to make was hard for any artist to struggle with, considering the largess of the media available and the fierce competition coming from every corner of the globe. Selling a work of art was even harder.

The paintings I had been doing in recent years had sold poorly. I wondered if the political and social issues I had tried to raise with my work might be the problem. In the arts, it often seemed that a sketch or an idea—usually abstract—won most competitions. A novel and exciting building design would win, but the win was determined without any earthly concern for practical things like a budget. The final product would have to be changed significantly from the initial concept to be built, and probably for the worse. I wanted to make a living but I wanted my concept to be concrete so that the execution would not destroy the poetry of the original idea. I didn't want to be forced to create some prosaic, watered-down version of what I wanted to express.

My finances were not great but they were not at a dangerous level yet. I was seriously considering a recent offer to teach an art class at a private school. As my artist friend Paul pointed out to me, it would only be for a few hours a week, and I could use the extra cash. There was also another consideration I now had to take into account. With no regular income, I would not be able to take Farah out on dates with the hope of winning her. I had to prove to her I could provide a good life for us.

I stood up and walked the length of my studio to look out the open window. It was a beautiful, warm July day with not a cloud in the sky. I thought of how nice it would be if, on a whim, I could pick up Farah and enjoy a long walk with her, hand in hand.

We had met as usual only a few days ago. As I was driving to the coffee shop, a favourite aria, from one of Mozart's opera buffa, *The Marriage of Figaro,* played on the radio. I sang along and tapped my fingers on the steering wheel in time. The uplifting music matched my positive mood, knowing I would soon see Farah again.

"Are you coming from your college classes?" I asked her after an exchange of pleasantries in the coffee shop.

"Yes, I am," she said.

"I'm guessing your interest in politics is more than just a passing fancy, then?"

"Yes, it is. But as I said before, I'm also interested in the visual arts, not to mention poetry, in particular the poems by Rumi."

"I must admit I've never read Rumi."

"Do yourself a favour and look him up. You will not be disappointed."

"Rest assured in the coming days I will do just that. What kind of visual arts do you prefer?"

"Art that is sociopolitical in nature, like Goya's *The Third of May*, Eugène Delacroix's *Liberty Leading the People* or Picasso's *Guernica*."

Her interests matched my own. I could feel my blood pressure spike in excitement.

"I'm also very taken with sociopolitical art," I said. "As a matter of fact, that's the kind of art I'm working on at the moment."

She took a sip of her tea.

"It would be great to see your work," she said and then looked away.

"You're more than welcome to come by my studio," I responded, overjoyed by her suggestion.

"Coming to your studio is not an option," she said and then turned to her political science textbook and started flipping the pages.

I wanted to talk more—her abrupt answer felt like a cover-up for a deeper issue—but her words *not an option* seemed to signal there was no room for further questions from me or explanations from her.

A few moments of awkward silence followed. My mind raced to find something to say, anything that would keep the conversation going. I wanted more time with her. The notion that I had known her before welled within me. Rationally, I was aware that I had only met her three and a half months ago. I really knew nothing about her. Yet already I felt closer to her than anyone I had known in all my life. When we were apart I missed the sound of her voice and the radiance of her smile. It would be a wonderful, unexpected gift if she had similar feelings for me. It seemed too much to hope for! Only time would tell if she found me interesting enough to want to know me in a more personal way.

I had dated dozens of women before I met Farah. I made love to them and then forgot them. I always hid my feelings from them. Something was always missing. A vast emptiness sat inside me unable to be filled—until I met Farah.

I took a deep breath.

"Then perhaps you would attend my next art opening?" I said.

"Sure, that would be fine," she replied.

I reached for my cup and spilled my tea over the table.

"Sorry about my clumsiness," I said, wiping the table with a napkin. "I couldn't begin to tell you what a pleasure it is for me to sit here and have tea with you."

"You seem like a nice person," she responded with a smile. "It certainly makes the time go by in a pleasant way."

"Does that mean we can do this on a regular basis?"

"If by chance I'm here, there's no reason why we can't have a tea together and talk," she said. "But I promise nothing."

"In that case I'll keep my fingers crossed," I said with a smile.

"Ha!" she said and pointed a finger at me. "Okay, you do that."

Farah's gesture had given me hope. Although she was careful not to openly show it, I detected a rising comfort level with me. But there still remained some secrecy and mystery in all she said and did. Nothing ever seemed straightforward. She piqued my curiosity and created a yearning to know her more that also heightened all my senses and my desire for her.

I drove home and tried working on a painting late into the night, but spent most of the time thinking about Farah. I wanted to keep the time I had spent with her alive. I wanted time to stand still. My love for her was enveloped in a desire to both possess and to surrender.

I went to bed feeling empty at the thought I would not see Farah for seven more days.

Eight

I STUDIED FARAH'S FACE FROM ACROSS THE TABLE IN SI-
lence. I hadn't seen her in a week. I couldn't get over the idea that
when I looked at her I felt as if I was looking at someone I knew
intimately. I tried to think of a safe topic for conversation.

"What kind of movies do you like?" I asked.

"Old movies and love stories with happy endings," she replied.

"Most people would find your taste old-fashioned and passé,"
I said.

"I couldn't care less if people found that laughable."

"Great attitude!"

"I don't even like to go shopping."

"You don't?"

"I don't!"

One more snippet of information revealed about her personal
life. She was normally mysteriously guarded. "I'd rather we talk
about something else," she would say.

Gathering the bits and pieces that she let slip without elabor-
ation, I was left with no big picture.

I wondered if her reticence to discuss herself was a mask
hiding another Farah, a part she kept safely encased behind a
protective wall. Sometimes she could be elusive. Other times she
could be ethereal and almost spectral. She had a beauty like no
other, which drove me mad with desire. The authoritative way

she carried her head and the effortless movements of her limbs struck me as full of self-confidence. She came across as detached, as though she were living in another dimension, a place I could never reach or be part of.

When she wanted my attention, a special look came over her face that was daring and beckoning, yet at the same time withdrawn, a kind of welcoming and keep-your-distance act. It made me wonder if she was truly interested in me or was in some way just teasing me.

At one Wednesday meeting over tea, curiosity got the better of me and I asked her, "Do you trust me?"

"Trust you?" She grinned curiously and teasingly at the same time. "I hardly know you."

"But you have trusted me enough to have tea with me many times over," I said. "Why not trust me now?"

"You have a point," she said.

I looked at her in a quizzical manner.

"Do you ever take any risks?" I asked.

"What kind of risks?" she said.

"Like, do you ever look at a man and secretly wonder what you could be missing?"

She gave a little laugh.

"What person doesn't occasionally look at the opposite sex? What are you getting at?"

"Does it worry you that life could go on the way it is now, the same, until you die? The same expectations, the same patterns—day after day?"

She fidgeted with a button on her blouse for a moment as if uncomfortable with my question.

"Well, you must take control of your life and make the most of it."

"Would you say, then, that you were happy with your life?"

She tucked a strand of her black hair behind her ear.

"Sure, I'd say I'm quite happy with my life."

The place was noisy with customers coming and going and talking loudly. I wasn't sure if I had understood her correctly.

"Don't you ever wish for something different?" I pressed. "Something that may be difficult to have but you want all the same?"

"Who doesn't occasionally?" Her eyes narrowed on me. "Why do you want to know what I want in life, anyway?"

I felt like I had stepped on her toes and stammered, "I-I barely know you and if you tell me, I-I'll know you better."

"Is that so?" she said.

I nodded.

"To what event do you give credit for the amazing person you—"

"Oh please!" She held up her hand as if to stop me from saying more. "I certainly don't consider myself amazing. If you see a bit of good in me, there is no particular event that made it so, aside from some intelligence and common sense I got from my parents and their love."

"It's great that you give your parents credit for the person you—"

"They taught me to live in the present and enjoy all that I do and all that life has to offer."

"It appears I have a lot to learn on how to best live life," I said.

"I'm sure you know how to best live life without me as an example."

I didn't want to say to her that my life was not the way I wished for it to be for fear she might think I was weak.

"Thank you for sharing your philosophy of life with me," I said.

"You're welcome. But as I have already said, you don't need help from me to know how to live your life."

"Well, let's just say I find you inspirational," I said.

"Thanks," she said. "I'm sorry to say it's time for me to go."

"I look forward to seeing you next week."

"Me too," she said.

Back at my studio I thought of our conversation. I was impressed with her comments. She had an admirable attitude towards life. I would be wise to work hard at being so positive. To show Farah that spending time with me was not a waste but something worthwhile.

I looked at the painting I had just completed. I had been working on it for a long time. Now that Farah was in my life, it was often difficult to concentrate on work, but I did manage it at intervals, particularly during those moments when I felt most vulnerable and the anxiety of wanting to be with Farah caused me pain. This pain was the engine that allowed me to bring to the surface my deepest feelings and to express them through art. Had the pain not been there, the creative energy would not have been as urgent. As far as my art and life were concerned, Farah was at once a detriment and a great blessing.

The finished work pleased me. But I typically felt good when a work was freshly complete, before sufficient time had passed to give me enough distance to look at it critically. On an easel next to it, an idea for my next painting had been partially transferred to a stretched canvas. With charcoal stick in hand, I looked at the drawing to see if anything needed to be added. I had collected a number of photographs of troubled areas in different countries.

Using aspects of these photos, I worked on an idea concerning discrimination, torture and other injustices taking place daily in many parts of the globe.

The quietness of my studio enticed me to work like I had when I was a child. When given a pencil to draw with, I could spend hours sketching without thinking of the time or the people around me. I found the beginning of a new idea full of promise and looked forward to seeing it come alive with the tip of my fingers.

I began work on the new painting in earnest.

Nine

ON THE SIX DAYS THAT I DIDN'T SEE FARAH I LIVED IN A persistent state of confusion. A constant emotional tug-of-war about her went on inside my head. It was midsummer and we had met and talked on numerous Wednesdays yet I still knew little about her and knew even less about what she thought of me. Despite all that, I loved spending time with her. Talking with her was like going on a journey of discovery without knowing the final destination. She captured my heart. The feelings I felt for her were as powerful as the feelings I had for art. It became evident to me that Farah had come to take precedence over the only thing I had loved since I was a boy.

The way her lips moved when her words rose in high notes denoting bursts of excitement touched me. Sometimes I closed my eyes and listened to the timbre of her voice and how she pronounced every syllable as if they were important notes in a musical composition. I fantasized about how she lived, what she ate, what she liked to do, what kind of friends she had. I even made up my own stories on those subjects.

I would win Farah's love. I would work at it like a galley slave. Even if the effort brought me nothing but discouragement and grief. I wondered if the relationship I had with Farah had been by accident or design. I had no idea. One thing was becoming evident—work in my studio may have been intermittent but it was also more expressive and raw. However, there were also days when I seemed unable to concentrate or even do the simplest of tasks.

My hunger for food had diminished. I was in constant turmoil about not only my financial situation, which would create difficulties in having a proper relationship because I could afford to spend little, but also with thoughts that she might already have a boyfriend, a boyfriend younger, more attractive and wealthier than me. My emotions fluctuated from moments of unbelievable happiness to total despair without warning.

Having lost interest in most things not related to Farah, I had avoided my two closest friends for months and finally agreed to meet them one night for drinks.

"There is something wrong with you," said Paul, an abstract painter, after we sat down at a local tavern.

"Yeah, what's happened to you?" said Dennis, a noted photographer.

"I have been busy as of late," I responded.

"We can see that," said Paul, as if he was officially the spokesperson for both of them. "We're busy, too, but still find time to get out."

"You're right," I said.

"Are you sure all is well with you?" said Dennis.

"All is fine," I replied." I've just been going through some things at the moment and it will take time to sort them out."

"I hope you're not hiding something from us." Paul raised an eyebrow. "If there is something wrong, you better come clean."

"Don't worry," I said. "Nothing is wrong."

I had no siblings and my parents died long ago. Paul and Dennis had become family to me. Paul was a tall, ruggedly handsome man of forty, with high cheekbones and dark hair. He could be mistaken for the Marlborough Man. His abstract paintings were full of energy and represented aspects of his personality in subtle ways. He could be rather hard when he criticized another artist's work, not from a place of meanness, but because of the effort he put into his own work. If he saw laziness in an artist's work, he named it.

One time, as we were walking through the Canadian Art section of the Art Gallery of Ontario gazing at some Group of Seven paintings, he turned to me and said, "Occasionally, when I look at this work, I think they learned how to paint by following instructions from one of those paint-by-number kits."

"Holy shit, Paul, that's a bit harsh, don't you think?" I said.

"Well, look at the faceted ways they painted, does that not remind you a bit of paint-by-number?"

"Would you say the same thing when looking at a canvas by the Fauvist painter André Derain?"

"Definitely not."

"But he paints in a kind of faceted way, with bold brushstrokes and vivid colours, does he not? What about the fact that the Group of Seven was attempting and to a great extent succeeded in distancing themselves from the European tradition of landscape painting? Is that not worthy of praise?" I said.

"I guess when you put it that way," he said with a pout.

Dennis couldn't be more different than Paul. He was forty-two years old and heavy, with a potbelly that shook when he laughed. He had a wide face with a medium-length beard that he stroked when thinking or under stress. His sense of humour—and smiling eyes when looking at someone—made him more attractive than upon first seeing him.

Dennis never went anywhere without his camera. For a long time the focus of his work was on classical gardens from countries throughout the world. But he was into portraiture now. In particular, he was concentrating on a series of portraits of homeless people. No matter where we went if he saw anyone "street-like" he would stop, walk up to the person, and ask them for permission to take their photo. He would explain he was doing it not to make money but as a way of recording the life of the city that most people refused to admit even existed. They usually allowed him to shoot.

I felt bad and even a bit dishonest in not letting Paul and Dennis in on my secret involvement with Farah. It just never seemed the right time to say anything. I wanted the situation to be more resolved first. Yet it was getting harder and harder to keep quiet. I knew that I would soon have to tell them.

"Listen, Vittorio," Dennis said. "From now on we are going to keep an eye on you and we will know if you are hiding something. There can be no more subterfuge. Do you hear?"

"Yes, I hear and promise to be an open book."

"That's all well and good," said Paul, "but we'll know if you are really on the up and up."

"Stop badgering me. Together, you two are like an over-protective mother."

"It's just what you deserve, behaving like you do," Paul said.

"Okay, let it be. I don't need policing."

"Dennis and I will be the judge of that," Paul said and pointed his finger at me.

"Okay, okay. What a pain in the ass you two are!"

"That's what friends are for," Dennis said with a laugh.

Ten

ONE MORNING, AS I LAY IN BED THINKING ABOUT FARAH, I remembered her saying that she liked poetry, especially Rumi. That day I went out and bought some books by her favourite poet.

Reading Rumi's beautiful words made it seem like Farah and I were walking hand in hand on a garden path. I felt like I was experiencing the same emotions she had felt when reading Rumi. It made me feel much closer to her.

The following Wednesday, we took a walk through a garden right off Lakeshore Boulevard. The place was beautifully kept with neatly cut grass and many flower beds in full bloom. We walked along the path at a leisurely pace and enjoyed the view.

"You once mentioned you like poetry."

"I do. Some of it."

"I do, too, especially Dante and his sonnets in *La Vita Nuova*. And Petrarch."

She leaned closer and narrowed her eyes. "I'm not familiar with *La Vita Nuova*. My favoured poems are by Rumi."

"I remember. I've been reading his poems lately. I must thank you for introducing Rumi to me."

Her eyes lit up.

"Do you like his poems?"

"Very much so."

"I've been reading his poems for a long time. I love them so much. I have even memorized a few. Would you like to hear one?"

"By all means."

Who looks out with my eyes?
What is the soul?
cannot stop asking.
If I could taste one sip of an answer,
I could break out of this prison of drunks.
I didn't come here of my own accord, and I can't
leave that way.
Whoever bought me here, will have to take me home.

Listening to Farah recite the poem was like hearing the sweetest music in the world.

"How beautiful and strange!" I said. "It's surprising that Rumi used words like *prison* and *drunkenness* to express human feelings."

"His imagery is surprising, particularly since alcohol was forbidden in Islam," she responded. "Nonetheless, he was fond of describing the sensation of being drunk and intoxicated with the ecstasy for his beloved. I believe the word *drunk* implies the bliss that is felt not so much in romantic love, but in a purely spiritual way, like the love for God. However, he also stated that we must first learn to love a human person in order to be able to love God."

"Well, it was beautiful."

Although other people walked on the garden path I had the feeling that no one existed except for the two of us. We sat on a big flat rock at the edge of the lake in silence.

"Have you ever been in love?"

Her question was so direct I was caught off guard. Never before had she uttered the word *love* in our conversations. I paused for a moment to come up with an answer and then said, "Once, when I was a teenager."

"How did that work out?"

Her directness again surprised me. I threw a stone and watched it skip along the surface of the lake. For a second, it brought back happy childhood memories.

"I don't think you want to hear about it," I said.

"Why not?"

"It's embarrassing to even think about let alone tell you what happened."

"Now you have me curious. How bad could it be?"

"You don't want to know."

"Please?"

"Sorry, not now, maybe next time when I see you."

On the way home I was encouraged by Farah's curiosity during our walk in the garden. I had hoped it indicated a willingness on her part to be more than just my friend. We were spending longer periods of time together when we met on Wednesdays. I took that to be a good sign. But I wanted to do something more to move it along. I would not be able to keep quiet about my feelings for her much longer. I had to tell her. She deserved to know.

When I got back to my studio late in the afternoon, instead of trying to force myself to paint, I decided to clean the place. I rearranged everything. By nine o'clock I was tired of cleaning and rearranging and called Dennis. I thought of telling him about Farah. I decided I would if the moment presented itself.

"Hey, what's going on?" I said when he answered his phone. "What are you up to?"

"Just looking through some photos I took."

"Are you telling me you're too busy to go out for a drink?"

"I didn't say that. I said I was looking through some recent work. I can come out for a drink, especially if you're treating," he said and laughed.

"Always the scrounger," I said jokingly. "Okay, the first drink is on me. What's Paul doing tonight?"

"He's out with Kathy."

We decided to meet at the Mambo Lounge on Danforth. It was a narrow bar but had a good ambience with live Cuban music and the occasional girl in a revealing outfit doing the mambo.

Soon after we arrived and ordered a drink, we were given maracas to play along with the live band.

"Hey, man," Dennis hollered over the loud music as he shook his maracas in my face. "You're often hiding from us these days."

"Yeah, life as a habit of getting in the way," I said and took a turn shaking my maracas in his face.

"I understand that but it's no excuse to ignore your friends. Are you working on something new? Is that taking up all your time?"

"I am working on a new painting which is giving me a bit of trouble. You know how it is."

"I do know but you seem more preoccupied than usual to me."

"No, not really, no more than usual."

I tried to keep a straight face so I wouldn't have to tell him about Farah. We were on our third round of drinks, feeling carefree, when the band started playing a song called "Mambo Italiano." I first heard the song sung by Dean Martin.

"This is it, man, do your thing," Dennis said and vigorously shook the maracas close to my face one more time.

"Stop that nonsense," I said and shook my finger at him. "No way am I doing that. Don't you dare do anything."

He waved at the dancing girl.

"No, Dennis," I hollered.

The girl made her way over. She had a big smile on her face and a sexy move. She took me by the hand, led me to the middle of the floor and started shaking her hips and dancing around me. I tried to follow as best I could, with much embarrassment, and listened to Dennis laughing over the loud music.

"I'm going to kill you if you ever do that again," I said when I got back to the table.

"Don't be such a wet blanket," he said.

"You've had your fun and I'm running out of money," I said. "Time to call it quits."

On our walk back home we both laughed as Dennis reenacted the pitiful way I had tried to dance on the sidewalk. He made it look so ridiculous that I laughed until my stomach muscles were sore.

For a brief moment, I had Farah out of my system.

Eleven

THE MONDAY AND TUESDAY BEFORE MY WEDNESDAY
meeting with Farah were always the hardest days of the week.
I tried to keep myself busy painting. But I rarely had much to
show for it.

In the car on my way to meet Farah at the coffee shop the
following week I thought about how careful she had been about
showing her feelings towards me. She was an intelligent woman
and surely knew by now that I wanted to be more than friends.
Perhaps she was waiting for me to make the first move—testing
me to see if I had the gumption to do it.

I decided I would take the plunge and let her know my feelings the moment we were alone together. I arrived a bit early and
waited in my car for Farah to arrive. We were supposed to go for a
walk. I started rehearsing how I would broach the subject. I kept
glancing at my watch and looking out the car window for her.
I was distracted and couldn't focus. She finally knocked on the
window, opened the door and settled into the seat next to mine.

"I was wondering if you would show up today," I said.

"I'm sure you have more important things to worry about,"
she said.

"That depends on one's point of view."

"True."

We drove to the Rhododendron Gardens on Lakeshore Boulevard. As we strolled along the garden path, I was anxious to get to the matter right away, but the knot in my stomach tightened so hard it threatened to suck the breath out of me.

"It's nice to be walking with you in a garden again," I said, not knowing how to start.

She smiled.

"Nice to be walking with you, too."

"We should make other arrangements," I blurted out.

Farah looked at me as if I had two heads.

"What are you talking about? Are you suggesting I'm doing something wrong?"

"Not at all. I-I-I'm trying to ask you out."

Her gaze transitioned from suspicion to wide-open awareness.

"Ask me out?"

"I'm asking you to go out with me."

"You mean on a date?"

"Yes."

"When did you decide to ask me that?"

"A while now."

"What does it mean?"

"That I'm very attracted to you."

She stopped walking and turned and looked at me.

"Did you realize just now that you were attracted to me? Or had you known before?"

"I knew from the moment I first laid eyes on you through the window of the coffee shop."

"Oh," she said in low voice.

She started walking along the path again as if to collect her thoughts.

"What compelled you to tell me now?"

"I could no longer keep my feelings to myself. The secret brings me no peace."

"What do you expect to get out of this?"

"The woman I've waited a long time for."

"You do realize that in waiting for the right woman, as you put it, you could remain on a waiting list for longer than you'd like?"

"Well, now that you point it out, yes, that could be the case."

"I don't know if you are implying what I think you are, but the capacity to love is not dependent on the right person coming along. It's dependent on you."

It was not the answer I had wanted to hear.

It was strange—the more I knew about her, the less I seemed to understand. I felt almost traumatized by the feelings I had towards her. How much more palatable love would be if I could build it like it was a clay sculpture, mould it into a shape that was meaningful and pleasing, or be able to relegate my effort back to the clay supply bin when things did not work out as they should have. Love was obviously not a work of art I could plan or make. There was no way I could simply try my hand one more time to see if I could be more successful. It didn't matter how difficult or inconvenient the love I felt for Farah might have been. I had to learn to live with it like an incurable disease.

I tried to convince myself that it was enough to have her all to myself for a few hours once a week. Only it wasn't. How wonderful it would be to walk with her any time I wanted, to see a movie with her, to hold her in my arms while she slept, to make love to her, to have a child together.

But once again she left me dangling like an apple on a tree wondering if it was ever going to be picked—or would I fall to the ground and rot?

Twelve

AS I WAITED TO SEE FARAH BETWEEN ONE WEEK AND THE next it was often difficult for me not to wonder if I had lost my sanity. It seemed like since meeting her I only lived for the next time I saw her. The measurement of time in my life was determined not by the cycle of the rising and setting sun but by my once-a-week meetings with Farah.

She had avoided giving me a straight answer at our last meeting. "I like you, too" or "I'm not interested in you in that way" would have been definitive. But she refused to indicate her feelings either way.

I had to find a way to win Farah's heart. I recalled she loved poetry so poetry was what I chose. I had read many of Rumi's poems since she first mentioned the poet. They were all beautiful. I chose just one that represented what I felt the first moment I saw her. I read the words out loud.

> The minute I heard my first love story
> I started looking for you, not knowing
> How blind that was
> Lovers don't finally meet somewhere
> They're in each other all along.

The simple words expressed deep feeling. It was as if Rumi had written the poem for me. Farah was inside me.

When Wednesday finally arrived I wore the newest jeans I owned with a light blue pinstriped shirt and pristine white sneakers. I admired myself in the mirror from different angles, trying to see myself as Farah might, and was pleased with the outfit I had chosen. It made me look younger, even kind of stylish, I thought. I hoped Farah would like it.

On the drive to the coffee shop I stopped at a flower store and purchased a single red rose to go with the poem that I had written out on good art paper. I hoped she would find my gift a pleasant surprise. I decided to bring her a red rose every time we met if she accepted this one. I ordered a chocolate glazed doughnut and returned to my car. I suddenly saw the parking lot in a different light. The knowledge that I had met Farah here made the ugly parking lot look much more agreeable. I began to see it as our garden. It seemed a safe place to me.

Farah pulled up and got out of her car. I watched the natural flow of her movements as she crossed the parking lot. She was the perfect picture of poetry in motion. She reminded me of the woman in Dante Gabriele Rosetti's painting *La Ghirlandata,* except Farah's hair was black and not red.

"Hello, beautiful lady," I said when she neared my car.

"Oh, hi," she said.

"How do you like our garden?" I said jokingly and pointed to the weeds in the parking lot.

She looked confused but then she caught on.

"It's beautiful," she said and laughed.

I presented her with the rose.

"Here's a rose from our garden," I said, "and to sweeten things, a chocolate glazed doughnut."

I handed her the doughnut and the rose. Around the stem of the rose I had wrapped the Rumi poem.

"Wow! That's very sweet of you," she said.

I held the car door open and she slipped in. I got settled in the driver's seat when she held the doughnut up to me and said, "Would you like a bite?"

"No thanks," I said.

She unwrapped the poem from the rose stem, bit into the doughnut, and silently read the poem. My breath slowed. She took another bite and left behind a tiny chocolate crumb stuck at the corner of her mouth. I longed to remove it with the gentle touch of my lips. She took another bite and then without looking up from the poem she placed the rest of the doughnut on the dashboard. My gaze fell on the half-eaten doughnut. I wanted to pick it up and bring it to my lips. I closed my eyes and dreamt of nibbling on it one morsel at a time while dreaming of the kiss we had never shared and maybe never would.

"Oh, how beautiful," she said and reached over and placed her hand on mine. "Thank you."

I took hold of her hand and gently squeezed it. I didn't want to let go. She pulled her hand away, as if we had done something wrong. I wrapped my other hand around the one she had touched. I wanted to hold the feeling. I longed to wrap my arms around her and feel her against me.

"Think nothing of it," I said with a wave of my hand. "Just a little thought, nothing more."

"Well, I love it," she said with a sparkle in her eye.

"I'm happy you do," I said.

She brushed the velvety petals of the blossom against her perfectly-shaped nose and inhaled. She closed her eyes as if she was being transported somewhere else by the sweet smell.

"Farah." I took a deep breath. "I would love to take you out on a date if you would allow it."

She opened her eyes and turned her head to face me. I searched her eyes and didn't see the positive response I had hoped for.

"Is that the reason you brought me a poem and a rose?" she said. "If this is your attempt at getting a date, I'm sorry for your trouble."

My heart sank a little, but I refused to give up.

"The rose and the poem were no trouble at all. As matter of fact, I learned a lot about Rumi. There's nothing to be sorry about. I honestly don't understand what you are referring to—"

"I'm married," she said, cutting me off. "I'm sorry."

I was left dumbstruck by her sudden announcement and wondered for a moment if she was joking.

"What?" I said.

She nodded.

"It is a fact. I am married. Because of that fact the chance of you and I going out on a date is pretty much nonexistent."

The news that Farah was married hit me with the force of a tsunami. It levelled my feelings and as it retreated, it dragged all it had demolished back out to sea, across the ocean of sorrow, with the same force with which it had arrived.

"You're married?" I asked one more time to make sure I'd heard right.

"I'm married," she said. "I'm sorry."

"But you don't wear a wedding band."

"I frequently don't because I always take it off when I do work in the house and I forget to put it back on," she said.

"But you look so young."

I was trying to come to grips with the shocking news.

"I might be older than you think," she said. "I'm thirty-five, actually."

I sank my head into my hands.

"I would never have believed it," I said when I came up for air. "You certainly don't show it."

She turned back, unsmiling, and faced the front.

"Well, thanks, I guess. I hope I didn't mislead you in some way."

"I thought your reticence was due to our differences in age. I'm fifty-five."

"I've never really thought about your age," she said. "I'm sorry about the situation. I understand it may not be what you had envisioned. I hope you don't think I've been taking advantage of you these past few months. That isn't the case. I truly enjoyed the time we have spent together. As a matter of fact, you've become a fixture in my life."

"Really? How so?"

"You are often in my thoughts when I'm at school, which makes it hard for me to concentrate. But being married allows me very little leeway in what I am allowed to do, no matter how I may feel."

"But I want you in my life," I said.

"That may be but I'm afraid the only relationship I can ever have with you is one without a physical...component. Please believe me when I tell you that you can love someone without the physical aspect. It's true. Physical attraction does not sustain love."

Her comments intrigued me. Farah had found words to set me on a different path. She began to talk about love in a way that was difficult for me to argue against. It left me hungry for more of her words.

"I understand that the intensity of emotion and physical attraction in a relationship is ultimately unsustainable," I said. "Physical attraction is in itself a shallow basis for a relationship.

But I have difficulty understanding how one can control the natural desire to physically want to make love to the person you want to be with."

"It's difficult but not impossible," she said almost immediately. "You have to think about love in a different way. If you want me to be in your life, it must be without the physical part. There can be no exception."

I focused on the words "not impossible" and clung to hope.

It was all I had.

Thirteen

MARRIED OR NOT, I YEARNED TO INHALE THE AIR FARAH breathed and occupy the space she walked. To smell the scent of her hair and graze my lips upon her silky smooth skin filled my dreams. In the many months I had known her I had yet to even hold her hand, let alone hug her, or give her a simple kiss on the cheek. Yet that didn't dampen my desire to see her. On the contrary, it made me want to be with her even more.

It was late September when a sense of dreariness came over me as I drove to Tim Hortons. Although the weather was still warm, the days were getting shorter. The landscape looked magnificent with the promise of autumn colours in the air, but the cooler morning air reminded me that winter was on the doorstep. Cold days were just around the corner.

When Farah arrived I gave her another rose.

"Do you want to go see an art show by my artist friend, Paul Savage, at the Art Gallery of Oakville in the Gairloch Gardens?" I asked.

"What kind of place is it?"

"A beautiful secluded place right on the shore of Lake Ontario and just minutes from downtown Oakville," I said. "It was a private residence at one time. As you will see, today it's a horticultural extravaganza. It's got lots of flowerbeds, manicured lawns and natural surroundings. I think you'll like it."

"Sure, let's go."

I watched Farah closely examine Paul's paintings when we got to the exhibition.

"How do you like my friend's work?" I asked her.

"I know nothing about abstract art, but I see a lot of emotion in these paintings, not only in the frenzied brushwork but in the warm colours he uses."

"They are full of passion. Paul is principally known for doing abstract paintings based on a nontraditional notion of the self-portrait. As you can see, they feature an abundant use of paint, with a hint of a human face about to appear on the surface of the painting, but it never does. It takes him many months to finish a painting, sometimes even years. The paint also costs a lot of money because he is not stingy in its use."

"That's very evident when one looks at the painting."

We walked out into the sunlight after seeing the exhibition. Numerous ducks and even some swans wandered on the mani-cured grass, behaving as if they owned the place. The roses bloomed in a blaze of colours. Farah stopped to have a look.

"Would you like to sit on the bench in the middle of the rose garden?" I asked.

"That would be nice."

My anxiety level started climbing as I thought about the questions I wanted to ask her.

"How do you like Gairloch Gardens?" I asked.

"The whole place is beautiful. This rose garden is fantastic. I'm amazed the roses still hold such beautiful blooms."

"Have you ever been here?"

"No. I had no idea this place existed. Thanks for bringing me here."

"It's my pleasure," I said.

I handed her a deep red rose, and as she smelled its velvet-like petals, I asked her, "How can a person fall in love with someone and not want to have physical contact with the person? I don't understand."

Farah turned her head and looked at me.

"If we made love in a physical way, the enchantment would be gone. Desirable as it may be, sex is a taboo we must not break or that special feeling we have for each other will be destroyed. The mystery and the aura of the forbidden will result in the pleasure also being destroyed."

I barely heard what she said. All I could think about was how she had confessed to having some sort of feelings for me, too. I stared into the dark depth of her eyes and managed to spit out, "I can't imagine a man and a woman being in love and not making love."

"Thoughts are very powerful and you must learn to control them if you are going to live a happy life," she said, staring at me. "As I have said before, if we are to have any kind of relationship, sex is out of the question. You must accept this fact or we cannot see each other again. Do you understand?"

"I'm not sure that I do," I said. "I think that all is possible if you love."

"Love is not about having sex or making demands. It's about giving. The moment a person makes demands, love ceases to exist and becomes an exchange like a business. I think you can agree that there's nothing more evident than the appearance of order in the universe. The vital part of that order is understood as being rooted in selflessness. The stars and planets don't move without taking into account what's around them. In human terms, considering others above our self, unconditionally, is the heart of our existence, and that is what I think the word *love* means."

Farah seemed to be suggesting a spiritual quest. As I considered her words she reached over and gently tapped my hand.

"Vittorio?" she said. "That is the only love that would mean something to me. All else is not love."

I swallowed hard when I realized the tips of her fingers still touched me. I longed to take her hand in mine but I dared not for fear she would pull hers away. So I remained still.

"Farah, what you said sounds beautiful, but is not physical love a part of sharing and giving in the most natural, intimate and human of ways?"

"Yes, but the act of sex is often put forth as loving and that is seldom true."

"I don't understand your reasoning."

"Well, in our situation, we are forced to rule out sex because of my marital status. In most cases, concentrating on sex destroys love anyway."

"Physical attraction has most often drawn people together and since time immemorial has acted as a door through which love blossoms," I responded.

"True, but if only the physical attraction is concentrated on, it mostly leads to carnal love. Sex leads to more unhappiness than its fleeting pleasures are worth. The easy attainment of love makes it of little value, while difficult attainment makes it prized. Every act of a lover should end in the thought of his beloved, as Rumi pointed out. In our situation, this couldn't be truer. We must learn to love each other with as much passion and even more passion than lovers who engage in sex."

Farah's words reminded me of the quip, "Sex is the consolation you have when you can't have love."

Although I found it difficult to accept that she would never have me in a physical way, I couldn't steer myself away from her. Perhaps I would find a strange kind of happiness through suffering never-ending longing and pain. I knew I shouldn't, yet I wanted Farah even more.

"I'm thinking about going abroad," I said to change the topic.

She pulled her hand away from mine.

"Really?" she said with a hint of excitement in her voice.

"It's just a thought for now," I said.

"Where are you thinking of going?"

"France."

"That would be great."

"I suppose so."

I reached out and touched her to get her attention.

"Farah, can I ask you something?"

"Sure."

"Can you love with passion without having sex?"

"I can. Can you?"

All the careful rehearsing I had done beforehand to say something deep and meaningful and convincing had escaped me. I didn't know how to respond.

We fell silent.

I knew I could not ask her to refrain from having sex with her husband. But what about me? Farah claimed to feel and know there was something better than sex—something higher. She wanted to remain free of the complicated entanglements that the act of having sex often brings. What happened to the theory that the more sex a couple had, the deeper their bond became? I fantasized about making love to her. I longed to touch and feel the smoothness of her skin. I dreamt of us being married.

Yet I decided in that moment that showing understanding and paying respect to Farah's ideas and needs would be the best way to win her heart. I found it difficult to imagine a relationship with the woman I loved without sex. But I would try.

"I'm not sure I totally understand," I said to Farah, "but being with you is the most important thing in my life and I will abide by your wishes as best I can."

Fourteen

ONE MORNING AT THE END OF NOVEMBER AS I PREPARED to meet with Farah at noon, I fussed with what I should wear. I looked out the window and saw winter was finally showing its face. A dusting of snow covered the streets below and blew every which way.

It was still early in the day. I pulled on my long overcoat, put my boots on and ventured out to buy a Christmas gift for Farah with the little money I had in my pocket. I knew she couldn't bring home anything that might cause suspicion and so I settled on *The Best Canadian Poetry*. The book featured a selection of fifty poems that critics thought represented the best and most vibrant verse in Canadian poetry. I hoped she would like it.

By the time I was ready to leave for our meeting, the light snowfall had turned heavy. But nothing was going to stop me from driving to the coffee shop to see Farah. On the highway the blowing snow made it difficult to negotiate the road. I got behind a snowplough and followed it at a snail's pace all the way to Tim Hortons. Cars with hefty amounts of snow on them sat in the parking lot blanketed in complete silence as if they had never existed in any other form before the snowfall. I searched for Farah's car and couldn't see it. I went inside the coffee shop and was glancing at my watch when I saw Farah push open the door.

"Hi," she said and smiled.

She headed to our usual table and placed her hat, coat and gloves on the back of the chair while I stood in line.

"I was worried that with this bad storm you might not show up today," I said when I reached our table.

"Thank you," she said when I handed her the cup of tea. "I was at school writing an exam and, honestly speaking, if it were not for that exam, I would not be here. It's dangerous to drive in this kind of weather."

"I suppose then I will have to thank Humber College for safely delivering you to me," I said with a smile.

"That's true."

"How do you think you did on your exam?" I asked.

"There were some rough parts, but I believe overall I did okay. We'll see when I get the results back. Wish me luck."

"I'm sure you did well. What are you doing over the holidays?"

"A lot of resting. I need sleep to recuperate. At some point I will also cut a Christmas tree, do a bit of decorating, and of course cook some special dishes."

"I only wish you and I could do that together," I said. "I know of a place where they have a bonfire and a team of horses that would pull us on a sleigh to where we would cut a tree. Afterwards, we would sit by the fire and drink hot chocolate. Wouldn't that be nice?"

I reached over and lightly touched her hand.

"That sounds great but as you know that can only be a dream," she said and wrinkled her forehead.

"I got you a Christmas present," I said.

I handed her the poetry book.

"How nice of you." She read the title and broke out in a smile. "I'm sure I'll enjoy the book. I'm sorry I didn't bring you a present."

"You brought yourself to me and that is the most precious gift I could possibly think of receiving."

"Thank you for the compliment, but I still feel bad at not having anything to give to you."

"With you at my side I have all I need."

She looked at me with a warm smile and touched my hand.

It was strange. Lately, whenever I thought of having sex with Farah, I felt guilty, as though wanting her physically was a betrayal.

"You are very kind," she said, still touching my hand.

"Do you have much time today?"

"Only enough time to enjoy tea with you."

"Will you be coming here over the Christmas holidays?"

"I will do my best to come see you. I'm sorry I can't be more certain."

"Be that as it may, I will still show up at our regular time in case you can make it."

"I promise to try. Again, I'm sorry."

"Do the best you can and I will be happy with that."

Fifteen

I DROVE TO THE COFFEE SHOP EVERY WEDNESDAY THAT December, in all kinds of weather, in the hope Farah might be there. I drank cup after cup of coffee and constantly looked out the window for her.

"Today she will come for sure," I would tell myself. "Wait a bit longer and you will be rewarded."

Each time she failed to arrive pained me. In those moments, the distance between Farah and me seemed so wide I wondered if the space between us could ever be bridged. In my desperation I convinced myself I had been deserted. What had she been doing instead of seeing me?

I tried to keep myself busy in the studio painting. I went to see movies I was not really interested in just to pass the time. I walked the streets of Toronto aimlessly, looking at people and window displays, but it all seemed a bit out of focus, like I was seeing things through someone else's eyes and not my own.

On Christmas day I drove to Paul and Kathy's house. They know I have no family and always invite me to their holiday dinner. A beautiful table was set. The turkey stood in the middle surrounded by roasted potatoes, carrots, squash, asparagus and cranberries. The wine flowed and the festive mood was in full bloom. Dennis, who had gone to visit a friend in Montreal and would not be back until after the New Year, couldn't make it.

The question—predictably—came up later in the evening.

"How has it been going with the women over the holidays?" Paul asked with a raised eyebrow.

I had to think of a quick answer that would not give too much away. "To be honest, I haven't seen much of anyone, other than a woman who is taking some courses at Humber College as a mature student, but since there is no school over the holidays, she is away, so there is nothing doing."

"Jesus, Vittorio, you are a dog for punishment," Paul said.

"What do you mean?"

"You always seem to pick the ones that give you problems."

"Don't be so mean," Kathy said. "No one has the power to plan who they fall in love with, just as was the case between you and me. It's an accident. When it happens, it happens, and no one can stop it."

"Thank you for the vote of confidence, Kathy. You are very kind and far more understanding than Paul."

"That's right!" she said and smiled at Paul.

He didn't like it when Kathy disagreed with him.

The holiday season finally came to a merciful end and January classes began. On the eve of our first Wednesday meeting in the New Year, I laid awake in bed for hours, unable to sleep, my head filled with a noise that pounded without pause. My mind had become stuck in the same groove, like a needle playing on a damaged record, repeating "Farah, Farah, Farah" over and over. It was like my mind had been hijacked and I was no longer responsible for my thoughts.

I got up early the next morning even though I was many hours away from meeting Farah. I paced up and down my studio, excited at the prospect of seeing her again.

Would she be as excited to see me?

I became overwhelmed with emotion when I saw her enter the coffee shop and jumped to my feet without thinking. Before Farah could even say hello, I hugged her and said, "You could not possibly know how happy I am to see you."

She smiled, looked around for a second, then looked back at me and said, "I'm happy to see you, too."

"I honestly thought the time would never pass," I said. "I missed you so much. I must confess I came by every week, not wanting to miss you in case you had been able to come."

"You knew there was no school and that it would be difficult for me to set aside time without creating suspicion."

"Just promise me that you will not miss one single Wednesday now that school has started."

"Vittorio, please. I try and do my best to be here every Wednesday."

On the slow drive back to my studio I thought about how nothing could make me happier than knowing for certain that Farah would show up every week.

"I'm happy to see you, too." I repeated her words over and over to myself. Then I remembered the stiffening of her body and the look she had given over her shoulder when I surprised her with the sudden hug—the implication that us being affectionate in public wasn't the right thing to do. It seemed like she was always on the lookout—always afraid someone she knew or someone who knew her husband might see us together.

I had hoped that something might have changed over the holidays. Despite the happy smile, and saying that she had missed me, the hesitation when I hugged her reminded me that nothing had changed at all.

Sixteen

ON A COLD SUNDAY AFTERNOON IN FEBRUARY, AS THE
wind howled outside and a cold draft seeped through my old
studio windows, I kept warm by straightening up the studio
and organizing my paints. Then I phoned Dennis and Paul and
got no answer. By four o'clock I was bored out of my mind and
poured myself a glass of wine. I thought about the teaching job
in downtown Toronto I had accepted. It would be a blessing to
have a bit of money coming in on a regular basis.

The school was located in an old Victorian house that had
once been the private residence of a wealthy family. It had a
raised front yard, held in place by a stone wall, and a short cement
walkway leading to the wooden steps of an open porch held up
by stubby Ionic columns and white-painted entablature. Inside
the front doors was a large hall with a high ceiling adorned with
thick crown mouldings. A beautiful oak staircase stood at the
end of the hall that led to the second floor. The staff office occupied a large room on the left-hand side of the main hall. On the
right was my assigned classroom, a small, rectangular room that
could fit ten to twelve students working at easels.

The pay wasn't great but it would buy groceries.

My painting class, designed for adult students of different
ages, was called "Intro to Painting" and took place Tuesday
evenings between seven and ten. I had ten students, a mixture

of men and women, and all were eager to learn how to paint. I introduced them to a variety of techniques and paint application methods so they could develop awareness of form and of how to achieve desired effects in their work. I chose to use still life arrangements for them to paint so they could investigate composition, tonal value, colour relationship, narrative and personal expression. University or college art classes sometimes attracted students who were looking only for the credit and showed little real interest in learning. My students were hungry to learn and seemed to appreciate any help they could get. I felt buoyed and optimistic.

One Tuesday evening, on the eve of my meeting with Farah, the class ended half an hour earlier than I had expected. That suited me fine because I had promised Dennis and Paul that I would join them at a bar called the Red Room on Spadina Avenue at eleven. Paul hinted I was in store for a surprise.

"All you do these days is mope around," he had said on the phone the previous day. "You need a change of scenery to perk you up and take you out of your doldrums."

By the time I returned to my studio it was almost ten. I had less than an hour to paint before meeting Dennis and Paul at the bar. I came up with an idea to solve a problem with the image I had been working on. I intermixed my painting strokes with thoughts of the problems between Farah and me. Other troubling aspects of our newly forming relationship aside from the rule of no physical contact had bubbled to the surface. Some were proving difficult to discuss and hurtful to both of us.

As a single older man I had experienced more relationships than Farah and now had a clear idea of what I wanted and needed in a relationship. The faces and names of the other women who had entered and left my life had become fuzzy. None had retained a spot in my heart. Farah was all I saw now—a woman who I had never kissed let alone made love to. The situation looked absurd. Still, I was older now, ready and willing to compromise when needed. But the no-sex rule was troubling. It sometimes made me wonder what Farah was looking for exactly. Was I just a guinea pig, an experiment of sorts for her, in the field of relationships? Was it all going to blow up in my face?

Falling in love with Farah felt like the most exciting and most dangerous thing I had ever done. The way it suddenly took over my life was madness. I experienced moments of panic, happiness, sadness and melancholy all in the same hour. I felt my personality was changing. I was willing to risk subordinating my identity to my love for Farah. My capacity for rational thought was under siege. Even art, the love of my life, had been relegated to second place—which truly scared me because I had never experienced a love so intense.

In my heart I wished for the unexpected—that our relationship would become physical. I was tired of the loneliness of my existence and filled with the hope of a love that would fulfil my life—and the object of this love was Farah.

I was willing to wait, hoping that she would one day turn to me and say, "Let's run off together." I kept looking forward to our next meeting with such hope and expectation in my heart.

I glanced at my watch and then dumped my brushes into a big jar of turpentine and left to meet Dennis and Paul. I entered the Red Room a few minutes past eleven. It took a while for my eyes to adjust to the dim light. The familiar smell of beer, hamburgers and french fries hung in the air like a cloud in the sky. The bar was noisy with talk and classic blues music.

With squinted eyes I scanned the room looking for a bald head in the crowd. Paul wasn't really bald. He actually had a full head of hair but on hearing his girlfriend, Kathy, say she had found a bald young man sexy, Paul shaved his head clean as a billiards ball. Kathy, in fact, was sitting with Paul when I spotted him at a table near the back of the bar with Dennis and another woman I didn't know. I wondered if the woman was the surprise for me. I was about to turn away when Paul called out "Vittorio, over here" and waved his hand in the air at me.

"Hello Paul, hello Kathy, hello Dennis," I said and gave Kathy a peck on the cheek.

"Well, you've finally shown your face, Vittorio," Kathy said.

"I've been busy," I said and looked away.

"I want you to meet my coworker, Jenny Adams," she said.

"Very pleased to meet you," I said and extended my hand.

"I'm pleased to meet you, too," she said. "I've heard so much about you."

"I hope some of it was good," I said with a smile.

"It was all good," she responded and gave me a slight wink.

I was glad I had put on my good jeans and a new shirt. Jenny was an attractive woman in her early forties with blue eyes and a pleasant smile on an oval face surrounded by long blonde hair. She wore tight jeans and a white blouse with the top two buttons left undone to reveal the top of her breasts.

I kicked Paul lightly under the table to let him know I was not pleased about the surprise. He looked at me as if to say, "What is wrong with you?"

The waiter arrived to take my order.

"What's your pleasure?" he asked.

"I'll have a Corona and a toasted BLT on brown, please."

"Coming right up. Do you people want a second round?"

"Maybe a bit later when Vittorio feels generous," Paul said with a grin.

"Here we go again," I said jokingly. "My name is not Diamond Jim," I pointed out.

"Well, you're working now and you have more money than us," Paul said.

"You're a barrel of laughs."

We sat there for a while eating and drinking and making small talk. Jenny occasionally touched my hand lightly as she explained what kind of work she did. I took it as a sign she was interested in me.

Paul took the hint and said, "The four of us should go on a night out."

"That would be great," Kathy and Jenny said at the same time.

"That would be nice," I agreed.

I was relieved when no date was suggested for the outing to take place.

Dennis noticed my relief and enjoying my discomfort he said, "You're a lucky man," and laughed until his belly shook.

"Shut the hell up, Dennis."

"Jesus, Vittorio, don't be such a pain in the ass."

"You know exactly what I mean," I said.

"Yeah, yeah. Just don't be miserable."

"It was nice to meet you," Jenny said to me as we were leaving the Red Room. "I hope to see you again soon."

"That would be great," I said.

The rest of us went to Paul's studio. We sat down and Paul poured wine for all of us.

"So, Vittorio," Kathy said and tapped me on the arm. "What have you been up to these days?"

I'm in love! almost slipped out of my mouth.

"Nothing out of the ordinary," I said. "Working in the studio as usual."

"Living with Paul, I should have known it was that," she said with a smirk on her face. "After all, that's all he does, too."

Kathy finished her glass of wine and stood up.

"I have to get up early in the morning for work and it's going to be a busy day tomorrow, so I'm turning in," she said. "Don't make too much noise and behave yourselves."

"Don't we always?" Paul said with a sweet smile on his face.

"It wouldn't be the first time you forgot to be considerate, especially after you've had some wine," Kathy said.

"Scouts honour," Paul said and got up and kissed her cheek. "Good night and sweet dreams, honey."

The moment she was out of the room Paul turned to me.

"What is wrong with you? Why did you kick me under the table at the Red Room?"

"Jesus Christ, Paul, you know I get embarrassed in situations like that. It always makes me feel like I'm cornered."

"He's only trying to help," Dennis said. "You should be happy we're worried about you."

"Didn't you find Jenny good-looking and pleasant?" Paul asked.

"She *is* good-looking and nice, too," I said.

"So what's the problem? You should think yourself lucky and worry only about the four of us going out on the town." Paul looked at me with raised eyebrows. "You are going out with us, aren't you?"

"Look, I appreciate what you guys are trying to do, but if I need help, I will ask you for it. As far as going out as a foursome, that isn't going to happen."

"I don't understand what's wrong with you. Dennis and I know there's something not right with you. What's bothering you lately? Out with it! It's time you came clean."

I took a sip of my wine. Dennis and Paul continued to stare at me with expectant faces. I finally decided I had better say something.

"I've fallen in love with a beautiful woman," I said.

"A-ha, now we see what's going on," Paul said.

"Wow!" Dennis said. "When did all this happen?"

"It's been a while now," I said.

"What's her name?" Paul asked.

"Farah."

"Why all the secrecy?" Dennis asked.

"Yeah, why?" Paul said.

I took another sip of wine. "She is attached."

"Attached?" Dennis said with a wave of his hand.

"Yes."

"Of all the good-looking women that have gone through your revolving door and you couldn't stick with any of them, you go falling in love with an attached woman?" Paul said. "Jesus Christ, Vittorio, you sure know how to pick them! Attached? What's so special about this woman?"

"I can't rightly say, but if you saw her with my eyes, you would understand."

"How are you going to work this thing out, genius?" Dennis said and lightly hit me on the arm.

"Well, that remains to be seen, but I'm sure, without a doubt, Farah is the one."

"I can hardly believe it," Paul said.

"At least now we understand your behaviour during these past few months," Dennis said. "Sometimes I thought you wanted to push us out of your life."

"Jesus, Dennis, are you out of your mind? You know you are the only people who I consider family. But, well,

I'm obsessed with this woman. That's why I've acted weird occasionally."

"It would be nice to meet this mysterious woman," Paul said.

"Well, if it all turns out well, you and Dennis will be the first people I introduce her to. Even though you guys are ugly, there's no one else in the world I would rather her meet than you two."

"Very funny, smart ass," Paul said.

When I was leaving Dennis put a hand on my shoulder and said, "Vittorio, I sure hope you know what you're doing and what you're getting into with this woman."

"Thanks for your concern," I said. "Have a good night."

Although I had told them Farah was the one, on the drive home I could not help feeling like Andromeda chained to a rock and wondered if fate would ever set me free as Perseus did for Andromeda. And would fate set Farah free? What unexpected event would allow me to be with Farah? It was daunting to think I might have to spend innumerable days, one after the other, waiting, and at the end there might be nothing.

In her resolve to stay true to her marriage vows, Farah appeared virtuous and unmoving. It almost made me want to abandon all hope. I had nothing to look forward to in a physical way, but I needed her, and because of it, I placed her high on a pedestal as a goddess. In doing so I moved her further away from me physically. Losing her was more frightening to me than never having the opportunity to be intimate with her.

"As long as you are married," I once told her, "we will never completely experience our full potential for happiness together."

"I'm truly sorry and I wish I could do more for you," she responded. "But if I leave him, he wouldn't be able to cope, and I don't want to hurt him in such a terrible way. We must learn to be happy with what we have. Please understand."

"I understand," I said. "But knowing that we can never be together in the way I envision is very painful."

"I feel bad, too, but what can I do?" she said. "Would you rather we had not met, or would you rather have met some other woman who could give you what you want?"

I thought about what she said and responded, "Having the companionship of the woman I love, even if only on an occasional basis, is better than not having you at all. But being the other man isn't easy. I'd love to be able to shout 'I love you' from the top of a mountain, but I can't tell anyone. No one knows what is going on inside me. I live like a shadow."

"Having to keep everything a secret isn't fun for me either," Farah said. "It's as sad and difficult for me as it is for you. How could I walk in the house and destroy his world? My husband and family don't suspect anything. They're not aware their lives could be turned upside down at any moment. Never mind the psychological damage it would do to my husband and the embarrassment he would suffer when people found out I had left him, my physical absence alone would kill him. I have a responsibility to my husband and father and mother. I already feel like I am committing a terrible crime against them when, technically, all I'm doing is having tea with you. I understand the difficulty in having a relationship such as ours, but we must find a way through the many obstacles in our path or we will end up with nothing."

It dawned on me that Farah had spent her entire life doing the right thing, looking after other people, making everyone happy.

It seemed she wasn't against having a physical relationship with me—she just didn't want to hurt so many other people in doing so. Perhaps she was seeking an affair based on support, understanding and validation, rather than sex. Farah had sacrificed so much for others.

I would also make sacrifices to win her over to me. It would be frustrating. I certainly knew how Sisyphus must have felt after having pushed the big boulder to the top of the mountain only to have it roll back down. Farah's husband offered her security, order and peace of mind. Perhaps she needed these things more than romantic love, which encompassed many highs and lows and a constant state of emotional upheaval.

"Love," she once pointed out, "is a desire for completeness and therefore addresses a deep human need. All of us are looking for the half of ourselves we are missing." She reached for my hand across the table and held it in her hand. Her touch was so unexpected I became overwhelmed and filled with desire. Then she quickly pulled her hand away.

Farah was in love with two men—her husband and me. Did we each fulfill different needs that one man alone could not? Did she see in her husband stability, discipline, calm and self-control? Did she see in me spontaneity, romanticism and a freedom that bordered on eroticism?

In having both of us, did she find not two halves, but one whole man?

Seventeen

I KEPT MYSELF AS BUSY AS POSSIBLE BETWEEN
Wednesdays to lessen the pain of Farah's absence. I mostly painted. But late at night, when everyone in the world was asleep and
I was confined to the silence inside my studio walls, the pain
would come back with ferociousness. I would lie in bed paralyzed
with a terrible, sinking feeling that I might not ever see Farah
again, and desperately hoped daylight would come and bring
relief to my suffering.

One morning, after another restless sleep because Wednesday
was still two days away, I woke up hungry, wanting a plate of
bacon, eggs and toast. I looked inside the fridge to retrieve the
items and was disappointed when I found no eggs, no bacon and
no bread. But I still had some butter.

"Shit!" I shouted out loud. "Now I have to go shopping in the
freezing weather if I want something to eat."

I was being careful lately with grocery buying so I could put
some money aside to treat Farah if the opportunity presented
itself. The only bit of splurging I allowed myself was the occasional bottle of wine to share with Dennis and Paul.

I threw my clothes on and rushed out of the building. A cold
March wind cut through me like the edge of a sharp knife. I
leaned into it with my head down and started walking along
Gerrard Street, headed to a Chinese grocery store near the corner

of Broadview Avenue. In the shop, a young woman and a little boy of four or five appeared to be having a problem understanding each other. The boy wouldn't listen to his mother. She chased after him as he raced around the store and wiggled his way out of her reach whenever she got near. He continued touching everything he could put his hands on—fruits and vegetables and toys and anything else that attracted his attention.

It seemed to me that the nicer the mother's manner was in trying to control the boy, the more the boy ignored her and the worse he behaved. I could see the mother was too much in love with the boy and as a consequence had little or no control. She couldn't reason with him.

The mother and son finally left and I paid for my groceries and exited the shop. As I walked home, I thought about the situation between Farah and me. When it came down to it, my approach with Farah in some ways resembled the little boy's mother with her son. I also let my heart be the master of my actions. Farah's sense of mystery had bewitched me. I found everything she said or did incredibly attractive. It reminded me of my childhood when my mother told me, "You are never to go into that room." From that moment on I was driven crazy by curiosity at what might be inside that room. It was impossible to go by the door without my mind going wild with the things I imagined to be hidden inside the forbidden room.

Farah was that forbidden room.

I imagined what she looked like naked, how I would make love to her, how my life would change if she were mine.

She became a sacred object of worship.

We did not go out on regular dates as normal couples do. Wednesday was the only day we set aside to meet. It was always secretive. Going to a movie or dance was out of the question. Someone might see us.

Each time we parted after our tea dates, I replayed the touch of her hand on mine a thousand times over so as not to forget what it felt like. Did she think about me as often as I thought about her? When my mind said no, I was filled with rejection and pain. The wounds my first love, Hope, had inflicted on me still hadn't healed. They lay open and raw as if they had happened only yesterday.

With Farah, I found meaning and beauty in doing simple things like drinking tea or taking a walk. It mattered not that it was an ordinary task. The extraordinary was next to me. The goodness I saw in her, like her wish to help people in need, was something I wanted to do in my own life. Through loving her I was made a better person.

I tried my best to understand her concept of what our love could be, but the idea of no sex never ceased to get in my way. Passionate love without sex seemed like doing a dance in which only she knew all the steps and rules. Try as I might to dance with fluid rhythm, I would remain at odds with the twists and turns and I would trip, step on her toes or simply be out of time with the music.

As we got to know each other more, I lived two complete and separate lives. In my normal life, I painted, ate, read, taught art part time and visited Dennis and Paul. In my other life with Farah, I lived inside a bubble in the wind, floating from one dream to another, wishing they would become a reality, hoping the bubble would burst and Farah would be at my side.

When I reached my studio apartment floor, I saw a man standing in the hall and knocking on my door.

"Can I help you?" I asked.

"My name is Tommie Chaves," he said with a smile and extended his hand to me.

He was an art collector who had come to see my work based on a recommendation by the curator of the Oakville gallery. He was a tall man dressed in black and sporting round rim glasses. We stepped inside my apartment and I offered him a glass of wine or cup of coffee.

"It's too early for wine, but I'll have a coffee, thank you," he said.

"My pleasure," I said and made him an espresso.

As he sipped on it, I began removing paintings from the rack and hung them individually on the wall. He looked at each work with great concentration and asked a question here and there.

"That one is fine," he said, pointing a finger at one of my larger paintings. "I'll purchase that one."

"One of my favoured works," I said.

I was overwhelmed with happiness at making a sale. After he left, I couldn't stop smiling. With a $15,000 cheque in my hand, I began thinking that perhaps a little distance from our everyday lives, or a geographic change, might provide Farah and me with a solution to our problem. A trip abroad, I concluded, would present us with a change of scenery to think straight about our relationship. I had the money now.

I decided on Paris. I hoped Farah would go with me. She would have to find an excuse for her husband.

Eighteen

I CALLED DENNIS AND PAUL AND INVITED THEM OVER for a drink, wanting to share some of my good fortune from the unexpected sale of my painting. I was ready for a night of music and talk about art and politics. It felt great to be able to buy an extra bottle of wine and not worry about how to pay the next month's rent.

"I need a drink, pronto," Paul said the moment he arrived.

"By the disgruntled look on your face, you most certainly look like you need one," said Dennis, who had already arrived. "What's going on?"

"I had an argument with Kathy."

"About what?" I asked.

"The usual—I'm not considerate enough. I'm self-centred. I don't spend enough time with her. I only care about my art."

"Is any of that true?" I asked.

"I'm an artist, like the two of you, and I have to do my work," Paul replied.

"Well, you can be an artist, but when you have a woman in your life, you must dedicate some time to pleasing her too or you will end up like me, having to spend my time with losers like you two," Dennis said with a frown on his face.

"You're a great comedian, Dennis, but don't quit your photography job or you might starve to death," I said.

I looked over at Paul. "There's no point in sitting there with a long face. Have another drink of wine and let's listen to some opera. It will cheer you up!"

"Are you out of your mind?" Paul said. "That stuff would depress me even more than I already am!"

"How about some Edith Piaf then, or Etta James or a taste of Chicago blues," Dennis suggested.

"That's more like it," Paul said. "Etta James would be fantastic."

"I just noticed your paintings," Dennis said. "Why are so many of them out?"

"Some guy was looking them over and bought one for $15,000," I said casually. "And," I continued, I've decided to spend the summer in France. Hopefully, it will clear my head and allow me to work undisturbed."

"You lucky dog!" Paul said.

"Good for you!" Dennis said.

"Does undisturbed mean you'll be going alone?" Paul asked.

"I'm going to ask Farah to accompany me. I have no idea what her answer will be."

"Hey, Dennis," Paul said and punched him gently on the arm. "I think our friend Vittorio has just joined the wealthiest percent of the population that captured the ninety-five percent of the post-financial crisis growth in the past few years."

"I believe you are right, Paul," Dennis responded. "For a socially conscious artist, he is sure widening the income disparity between himself and us."

"All the more reason to drink his wine." Paul laughed and reached for the bottle to fill our glasses. "He can afford it now!"

"Jealousy will get you guys nowhere," I said and gave them the finger with a smile on my face. "So eat your heart out."

Dennis started to sing "At Last" along with Etta James. I watched him and got a kick out of seeing how earnestly he tried. I tapped Paul on the arm and said "Let's show Caruso here how it's really done" and we began to sing at full volume.

"How did you like that, Dennis?" I said when the song ended.

"Losers! You two managed to ruin the song." He slid his empty glass my way. "Make yourself useful and fill my glass."

"Fill it yourself," I said.

He grunted as he reached for the bottle of wine and filled his glass to the rim.

"Jesus, Dennis, you're pretty free with that wine," I said and laughed.

"You just made a shitload of money," he responded. "Don't be stingy over a bit of wine."

Etta James started singing "Trust In Me." We sat sipping wine and listening to her dramatic rendition of the song.

Paul put a hand on my shoulder.

"Vittorio, do you trust this Farah?"

"I do trust her," I said. "But I still don't know what will take place down the road."

"By the way, Vittorio," Dennis said, "what do you plan to do with your studio while you're away over the summer?"

"Sublet it," I said.

"I think I know someone who might be interested," Dennis said.

"In that case, here's an extra key." I got up and took it out of the drawer. "That would be fantastic if you did. Thanks."

The next Wednesday, I told Farah about the sale of my painting, and that I planned to use some of the proceeds to travel to Paris for the summer.

"Please come with me," I pleaded.

"I am so happy about the sale of your work but going to Paris with you would be difficult, to say the least," she responded.

On the last Wednesday in April I jumped in my car to meet Farah one final time before my departure and to again ask her to travel to Paris with me. I had continued meeting her every week since my painting had sold and I had decided to spend the summer in France, and continued to ask her to join me, with no success. Now, one last time, I would do my very best to convince her to go with me. It was my final chance.

I had two presents in the car to give Farah—a book on the symbols of art and a poem called "You Are My Garden" that I wrote on good art paper with her in mind.

> This rose that I bring you
> It's not simply a rose
> But all the beauty I see in you
> Among its petals
> Are the thoughts I have of you
> Which I no longer wish to hide
> This rose allows me to say
> The warmth of your smile lifts my spirits
> You help me to grow and blossom alongside you
> You fill my heart with wonder
> You are my garden
> I hope to be your sun.

I stopped by a flower boutique on my way to the coffee shop and bought a single rose. When I got to the parking lot I placed the poem in the book, wrapped it in paper and tied it with a bow. I was standing by my car when Farah's car pulled up beside mine. She got out and gave me a quick hug while looking over her shoulder. Then we got into my car.

"Oh Farah, I'm so happy to see you. How are you? How was your week?"

"I'm fine. My week was not bad. I had a lot of reading to do for school and not all of it interesting."

"Studying is like painting a picture," I said. "You spend a lot of time cleaning the brushes and that's no fun, but it's necessary, if not enjoyable."

"I never heard anyone put it that way before," she said with a smile.

"As you already know, I leave for Paris in two days' time, and my dream is that you will join me there," I said. "There is no other person who I would rather be there with than you."

"Oh, my dear Vittorio!" she cried out. "Spending time with you doesn't feel wrong, it feels right, but going to Paris with you is not an option."

"Please come," I said.

"I can't!" She frowned. "I'm not happy you're going, but considering the pressures we both feel under, it might be a good idea to have some distance between us and it might allow us to think more clearly. It could be good for your art, too."

"If I go alone, what will happen to us?"

"What we have between us won't evaporate just because you're away. If it does, then it wasn't meant to be."

I didn't share her optimism.

"Spending the summer in the City of Love without the person I love seems very odd," I said.

"I'll still be here when you come back. It could be good for you. You'll discover new and exciting things."

"Maybe so, but without you, I will find no pleasure in it."

"That's just not possible."

We fell silent and stared out the windshield as if trying to catch a glimpse of our future.

"I have a gift for you," I finally said. "Don't open it until I'm in Paris."

"Thank you," she said. "I have something for you, too."

"I'm touched," I said.

"It has nothing to do with you going away. I've wanted you to have something of mine for a while now that I thought you might cherish."

She reached inside her coat pocket and took out a small square box wrapped in red paper.

"Here," she said and handed it to me.

I stared down at it.

"Promise not to open it until you arrive in Paris. Then we'll both have gifts to open," she said. "Please don't ask me for my phone number. I don't want contact with you while you're away. We both need time to reflect. We will talk when you come back."

"Are you sure that's what you want?" I said trying to stop tears from welling up.

"I'm sure."

She reached her arms out to me. I met her embrace and held her tight, wishing we could stay like that forever. I felt the beat of her heart against my chest and the warmth of her flesh where it touched mine.

Then she backed away. A sudden chill seemed to settle into the space between us.

"I'm sorry, Vittorio, but I must go," she said.

We got out of my car and headed towards hers. I was filled with mixed emotions. On the one hand, I was excited about the prospect of spending four months in Paris. On the other hand, I was saddened at what could happen to us during my absence. She stood in front of me when we reached her car and gently placed her hands on the sides of my cheeks.

"You matter," she said and then got into the driver's seat and drove off.

Nineteen

TWO WEEKS HAD PASSED SINCE I ARRIVED IN PARIS AND although I saw many beautiful things nothing had fired up my imagination for a new art project. It felt like a big boulder blocked the road I was travelling on and I couldn't see a way around it. Perhaps only a bulldozer could clear the path.

The whiteness of the paper in front of me looked daunting.

Now that I had all this time on my hands to do what I loved the most, I should have been in love with the potential of the blank sheet of paper. Was that not the way great artists looked at their materials? Where most people saw paper, canvas, marble, a piece of scrap, cloth or stone, an artist saw these things as drawings, paintings or sculptures before they were even created.

Why was I not able to see life in the paper in front of me?

It was Farah, of course.

Given that she was in Canada and I in France, and we had no communication, I felt like I was living in a vacuum. I hoped this was not to be a mirror of my future, with us further apart, and me increasingly lonelier. In her absence my love for her had only intensified, the pain hurting so much on some days that I wished her gone from my mind—but there she remained, unmovable, like a distant mountain. A future with her hinged on a hope, and if choosing Farah meant losing myself and all the important things that had mattered to me before I had known her, then I would choose Farah.

"Draw first, think later," I said out loud.

But I couldn't fill the blank page with anything. Exasperated, I decided to go out for a walk in the hope of finding inspiration. I reached for the kerchief Farah had given me and placed it inside my coat pocket—hoping it might inspire me. I grabbed a pencil and my leather-bound sketchbook and left the studio.

I walked along the wide sidewalk of Quai de Gesvres, a congested, busy road that runs alongside the Seine, past bookstalls made of green plywood. With luck and patience, one could discover a real treasure in one of them, a book or one of the many posters and tourist trinkets they sold. I crossed Pont Marie, walked along Rue des Deux Ponts, crossed Pont de la Tournelle, then made a right on Quai de la Tournelle.

I arrived at Pont de l'Archevêché, the bridge that spans the Seine just behind Notre-Dame, made famous for the thousands of "love padlocks" adorning its metal banisters to represent everlasting love. I saw couples kiss and fasten their locks to the bridge. I watched them use both their hands in a sweeping motion to heave the key over the banister into the current of the Seine, thus sealing their love for all time.

A young man with an arm full of locks approached. I carefully eyed the different sizes and then bought one. With the key, I scratched the initials *F & V*, for Farah and Vittorio, into the metal. When I finished, I held the lock to my heart for a moment before fastening it to the bridge, and then reached inside my coat pocket to touch the kerchief.

"This is for us," I said out loud and promptly cast the key into the Seine. I heard it hit the water with a plop. Now, according to popular belief, our love would remain unbroken.

From the bridge I saw the flying buttresses of Notre-Dame extending from the side and back of the building. A jolt of excitement leapt through me as I made my way to my next destination. As I walked alongside the cathedral, I marvelled at the functional characteristic of Notre-Dame's flying buttresses. They weren't solidly attached to the building like traditional buttresses and as a consequence transmitted the lateral forces across the span of intervening space between the wall and the pier. It reminded me of a beautiful dinosaur skeleton leaping from the side of the building with unparalleled grace.

I reached Notre-Dame Square and stood in awe. The beautiful limestone facade gleamed so brightly in the sunlight I was forced to squint to look at it. Its composition was a harmonious ensemble based on a play between vertical and horizontal lines. The beautiful portals, with their wrought-iron strap hinges and arabesques, were surrounded by sculptures. I studied the carvings on the portals—a menagerie of figures representing a vision of the Last Judgment. The figures are guided by angels, directing them to the places reserved specifically for them in accordance with the kind of lives they had lived on earth. Christ sits majestically at the centre of the tympanum, the wounds on his hands, feet and side clearly visible. Two angels at his side carry the *Instruments of the Passion*. The impressive rose window, high on the façade, crowns the tympanum.

I sat on the sidewall at the periphery of the square, observing the reaction of the many visitors, their heads turned upward to the heights of the cathedral, eyes wide open in wonderment. I reached for my pencil and sketchbook and began to draw. After finishing a sketch, I took one more look at the cathedral façade and then went back to the drawing I'd just done and next to it I wrote:

My dearest Farah,
Here is an image of Notre-Dame as I saw it while standing in front of it. With the drawing, I have also added a little poem so you will have a better idea of how beautiful Notre-Dame is.

P.S. Wish you were here!

Vittorio

OUR LADY OF NOTRE-DAME

Our Lady of Notre-Dame
With the gleaming facade
How beautiful you are
All dressed in white
Your bells ringing
Calling the faithful to prayer
Quasimodo milling about
Pining for Esmeralda
Atop the bell fry
From the depths of his cell
He rings the bells
Will Esmeralda hear them wail?

I closed my sketchbook and raised my eyes to the cathedral façade to take in its splendour one more time. I thought there must be something in the nature of a rational being to covet a beautiful sight, not just the physical, which is only animalistic, but also to the intellectual in a marriage of the spiritual and physical.

I glanced at my watch and saw that it was one o'clock. I decided to have lunch at the Latin Quarter. Two arteries, Boulevard St. Germain and Boulevard St. Michel, bisect the area. Hundreds of crooked streets run off these boulevards, not unlike the roots from the base of a tree. Myriad restaurants and shops packed with visitors lined the narrow cobblestone streets.

I stopped at a café on Rue Mouffetard, a typical pedestrian street in Paris. The moment I sat at a table the aroma of roasted chicken hit my nostrils and sharpened my appetite. I ordered it with a salad and glass of wine.

The Latin Quarter has largely been gentrified. Sitting in the cafe watching people stroll by brought to mind the days when the street was full of students, writers and artists, mingling at all hours of the day and night, exchanging ideas and discussing the politics of the day.

I finished lunch and then decided to take the Metro to the Musé National Eugéne Delacroix, in the heart of Paris. The studio contained personal memorabilia of the artist along with a collection of paintings, drawings, furniture and engravings. The dark red-painted studio also showcased his easel, palettes, painting tables, glazed pottery and the glass which he used to wash his brushes in. The large studio windows looked out onto a charming garden, which was kept as Delacroix had designed it. I could feel the spirit of Delacroix permeating the air as I walked around his studio and got goosebumps.

I left the Delacroix studio and crossed Pont Des Arts to the Louvre. I spent the rest of the day in the French Art area, where I enjoyed many of the great paintings I saw but found the greatest enjoyment in watching visitors' reaction upon their first encounter with the 1571 portrait of *Gabrielle d'Estrées and One of Her Sisters* by the artist Francois Clouet. The two sisters sit in a bathtub with one sister pinching the nipple of the other sister. The gesture gives the image a heightened quality of eroticism, which is also reinforced by a semi-nude painting hanging above a fireplace in the background behind the two sisters. Tourists often stumble upon the painting and come to a sudden stop, eyes wide and mouths agape, to gawk at it. They point to the image and whisper, and then look over their shoulders, almost afraid of being overheard or perhaps thinking their comments risqué or less than acceptable in a place like a museum.

I walked along Rue Rivoli after leaving the Louvre and stopped at a depanneur to buy a bottle of wine. It was around eight by the time I returned to my studio. I felt a bit tired from all the museum visiting. I decided to lie down before I made dinner and fell into a deep sleep.

Twenty

I WOKE UP AT DAWN TO THE SOUND OF RAIN SPLAT-
tering against the windows and could not find my way back
to sleep. I got up, poured a shot of brandy into a tumbler, and
climbed back into bed. I leaned my head against the wall and
looked aimlessly around the room. Stomach growls reminded me
that I hadn't eaten dinner the previous evening. I ignored my
hunger pangs and took a sip of the brandy.

As I listened to the rhythm of the rain hitting the glass, I
wondered if it was raining in Toronto and if it had awakened
Farah. I imagined her and her husband in bed. Did they just
finish making love? Did he take her passionately? Did she moan
with pleasure as I would if she had been with me? I swallowed the
last bit of brandy and closed my eyes.

I rose and performed my usual morning duties—shower,
shave and teeth brushing—and then reached for the espresso. I
found the coffee can empty. I threw on some clothes and went
out to the depanneur.

On my way, I stopped to check the mailbox and discovered a
postcard from Dennis and Paul. On the front was a picture of the
CN Tower. On the back they had written:

Hello, Vittorio.
How's it going in Paris?

We suppose, by now, parlez-vous français, and
no longer care to converse in English. Ha! Ha!
Since you have the misfortune of having to look
at the Eiffel Tower all the time, we thought you
would like to contemplate "la tour CN," as it is
a great sight for sore eyes. All jokes aside, just
want you to know all is fine with the rental of
your studio. We will look after things here so
have a great time.
Cheers,
Dennis

P.S. Paul wants to know how you are doing with
the Parisian women. He says for you to break a
leg. Ha! Ha!

It was a particularly grey day and the postcard from my friends
lifted my spirits. I carried on to the depanneur, purchased coffee,
and returned to the studio. The raindrops on the studio window
blurred the world outside and left me feeling more lonely than
usual. I wished Farah was at my side. I decided to write a poem
to her so I would feel her presence, and although I had brought
back coffee, I decided instead to make tea, thinking Farah might
be drinking one at the same time.

I took the cup to the drawing table. The white pages of the
sketchbook glared at me, challenging me to start the first sen-
tence, the first word, the first anything.

Two hours passed and I had scratched out every word put to
paper. Frustrated and lonelier than when I started, I decided to
simply write Farah a letter.

My dearest and most beautiful Farah,

I hope you do not find it presumptuous if I address you as "my dearest and most beautiful Farah." I think of both you and of your name as most beautiful, so please take it as a compliment.

It's a dreary day in Paris and I'm feeling out of sorts, mostly lonely and a bit sad. I started wanting to write you a poem, but verse failed me, which goes to show you that I am no poet. So I've turned to writing you a letter instead.

Yesterday, I travelled to the city of Angers to view tapestries that depict the struggle between good and evil, with the wellness of humankind at stake. If only you had been with me! I kept touching the kerchief you gave me so I could feel your presence next to my heart.

The first was *The Apocalypse Tapestry* at Château d'Angers. I have no idea if you know of it but *The Apocalypse Tapestry* has survived from the fourteenth century. It is the oldest existing medieval French tapestry. Immense—woven in six sections that each measure six metres high and almost twenty-four metres wide—it tells the story of "The Apocalypse (Revelation of Saint John the Divine)," a book from the New Testament—the struggle between God and Satan. My encounter with the tapestry was esthetically shocking. Scenes of the apocalypse, woven into backgrounds of deep blue or fiery red, hung in a dark blue hall that seemed to extend forever, with low lighting that added to the drama of the imagery.

It sets your imagination on fire.

I imagined myself standing with my arm around your waist, both of us enthralled by the apocalyptic vision, unable to speak for its power.

I imagined holding your hand as we walked out of the Château and crossed the bridge that leads to the Saint Jean Hospital, which houses a second tapestry set, created as a tribute to *The Apocalypse Tapestry*.

I imagined how you would have loved *Le Chant du Monde (Song of the World)*, its vivid colours contrasting against a black background, and its socially conscious creator, Jean-Lurçat, who desired to create a contemporary expression of the final victory of good over evil, of man living in harmony with the world and its elements.

How I loved these works, Farah, and how I would have loved to tour them with you by my side. I would also love to share their every detail in this letter, but I must bring it to an end here, before I scare you off with too many words.

Yours ever loving,

Vittorio

P.S. I MISS YOU.

It was midafternoon by the time I finished writing the letter. Time had passed without my noticing it. I closed the sketchbook, stretched my arms to loosen my muscles, and decided to go out to purchase a postcard to send to my friends in Toronto.

In a depanneur I came across a postcard with an image of *L'Origine du Monde,* a painting by Gustave Courbet, which shows a surprising view of a woman's torso, her thighs spread, forcing the viewer to look directly at the woman's vagina. It was painted more than one hundred and fifty years ago and still retains the power to provoke. On the back of the postcard I wrote:

> My dear friends Dennis and Paul,
>
> Thank you so much for looking after things for me. You are the best friends one could possibly hope to have. I must tell you, though, that as far as missing and contemplating the CN Tower is concerned, you can keep it for your own use. I will not venture to say what that is but I think you can imagine it. Ha! Ha!
>
> The image on the front of this postcard is what I am concentrating on now. I think it's much more engaging than the CN Tower, but to each his own. And yes, Parisian women, as you can see, are awesome!
>
> Cheers,
>
> Vittorio
>
> P.S. The wine is fantastic and also cheap! Eat your little hearts out. Losers!

I left the studio and mailed the postcard. The rain had stopped and the sun peeked out from behind the clouds. I started along Rue des Deux Ponts back to my studio and was about to cross Pont Marie when I heard the sound of music that seemed to be coming from somewhere along Quai de Bourbon. I followed the sound and after a short walk, I came upon a band playing in a little square carved out at the side of the road.

From my vantage point, I could look across the Seine and see the sandy riverbank beaches that the citizens of Paris enjoy as much as the French who live near the sea enjoy the sandy beaches. Whole families spend time there enjoying picnics, riding bikes, drinking coffee or a glass of wine or simply strolling along the walkways. I could also see my studio building, as well as the spire and lantern of l'Hôtel de Ville rising above the treetops.

The band played all sorts of dancing music—from Viennese waltzes and salsa to jazz. Some people milled about listening to the music. Some danced. The scene brought a smile to my face as there is nothing like listening to live music in the open air in the city of Paris. The romanticism often associated with the city couldn't have been more evident than at that moment. I couldn't imagine such a spontaneous musical concert breaking out in any other city. I danced with total strangers as if I had known them all my life. I couldn't tear myself away from the spot.

Finally, I sat alone. I watched the lingering rays of the sun diminish from a low stone wall at the periphery of the square and then vanish beyond the buildings across the Seine.

If only Farah was with me.

Twenty-One

I RETURNED TO THE STUDIO AND WENT TO BED AND thought about my life before Farah. I had been unhappy for a long time. I had a deep hunger to love and to be loved, and to give love and to receive love. I knew I had found it the moment I saw Farah. I didn't really know how Farah felt about me.

"You must learn to find happiness within yourself and not depend on other people to provide it for you," she had told me.

It was not a reassuring declaration of her love.

It was hard to believe that a chance glance through a window of a coffee shop had the power to divert the course of my life in such a dramatic way. What would happen when I got back to Toronto? Would she leave her husband for me? What was she doing at this very moment?

I reached for the box she had given me. I opened it and removed her kerchief. I fingered the silk kerchief lightly and then brought it to my nose, breathing in her scent that still lingered on the delicate fabric. Her lock of hair hidden between the folds fell into my palm. I brushed it against the tingling flesh of my cheek. I felt magically connected to her in some way and hoped she could sense me close to her.

Farah often visited me in my dreams. She came in silence, almost as if floating on air, and dissolved like mist in the sun when she left. She would lie at my side without making a sound and press her warm body against mine. I would wake up, shivering with desire, and extend my arm to the other side of the bed, only to find it empty. Then I would lie with tears in my eyes, as memories of us poured forth. I wondered if she thought of me, if she missed me, or if she was so occupied with living her life that she had forgotten I ever existed.

Perhaps she hadn't been wrong after all when she said, "If the object of our relationship is purely physical, as in sexual desire, the soul cannot make contact and love cannot be born."

Did my soul reach out to her in ways it never would if we had made physical love? I concentrated for a moment on the pull deep within me, the warmth and longing, on a love so great that it surpassed all the love I had ever felt before. Is this what Farah meant?

I decided to get out of bed and work on an art project to get Farah out of my head. I set the radio to a classical music station and started sifting through a bunch of photos I had taken in the hope that an idea would come to mind. A photo I had taken of a young woman playing the cello sparked my curiosity. In looking at the image, I could still hear Beethoven's music from his third sonata, the interweaving passages moving from the piano to the cello created an arresting and beautiful conversation, the melody pleasing to both the mind and the ear. I've always loved the cello, not simply for its romantic and sexual connotations, given its shape of the female figure, but for how it evoked the human voice. The photo reminded me of a work by Man Ray who painted the F-holes of the string instrument on a photo of a woman's back in his work *Le Violon d'Ingres*.

I reached for a sheet of paper and began drawing parts of the cello, starting with the scroll and tuning pegs, as they have a beautiful baroque quality and sensuous movement. I lightly sketched the general mass and shapes of the scroll, then applied greater pressure with the pencil, and created darker lines as I established its final placement. Wanting the viewer to see my thinking process, I refrained from using an eraser and left the initial sketchy lines as evidence. I drew without worrying where it would take me. Many hours later I had half a dozen drawings. In looking at them I realized I still had no concrete idea where I was going. But I was satisfied I had spent the afternoon working with such intensity that I had even forgotten to eat dinner.

I hung the drawings on the wall so I could look at them in the future with a fresh eye.

Twenty-Two

DAY AFTER DAY IN MY PARIS STUDIO APARTMENT I TRIED to make art but failed to create anything worthwhile. It got so depressing that on some mornings, when I opened my eyes, I felt like closing them again and going back to sleep. I needed to make a change in the hope it would unlock my imagination.

One morning I got up earlier than usual determined to accomplish something. I showered and shaved and then mulled over where to visit as I ate toast and drank espresso. I couldn't make up my mind and decided to just take a walk. I exited my studio and ran into André, an artist who lived just down the hall from me, who I rarely saw. He was always pleasant and liked to chat when I did see him.

"Bonjour, André. You're early this morning," I said.

"Bonjour, Vittorio. How is your stay in Paris?"

"Four weeks in town and I have nothing to show for it!" I said.

"Mon Dieu!" André said and raised an eyebrow. "You mean to tell me you've done nothing these past four weeks? Ce n'est pas possible. Paris has everything you could wish for. I'm surprised you say you have done nothing."

"I've done some drawing, but nothing of substance. I need something to sink my teeth in and to shake me up," I said with a chuckle. "Hopefully I won't have to resort to selling my soul to the devil like Faust."

André had a good laugh and placed his hand on my shoulder.

"Yes, I am well aware of Faust, but Vittorio, before selling your soul to the Devil, you ought to visit the Paris catacombs. Or have you been there already?"

"No," I replied, surprised Paris had catacombs.

"You might find something there to move you into action."

"Catacombs?" I repeated.

I feared I had misunderstood him.

"Yes, catacombs," he said. "But not like the ones in Rome. The Paris catacombs are filled with millions of dead people."

"Really?!"

"Yes."

Intrigued by the thought of millions of people buried under the streets of Paris, though the very idea seemed improbable, I decided to go and see for myself.

"Thanks for the tip," I said.

"If you are going there you'd better hurry because the place is busy," André said. "Good hunting. Hopefully you'll find something to inspire you. Au revoir mes amis."

"Au revoir."

I returned to my studio, gathered my camera, sketchbook and Farah's kerchief, and headed directly to the metro to purchase a ticket for Place Denfert-Rochereau. I wanted to be first in line because André said the lineup to enter the catacombs was often long.

I arrived at nine, an hour before it opened, and the line already stretched far beyond the main entrance. An hour and a half later, I finally made it to the kiosk, where I paid the twelve euros entrance fee and was directed toward a circular stone staircase that led down into the catacombs. As I made my way deeper beneath the city, only the hollow sounding footsteps of other visitors walking behind me and the gurgle of water running beneath me broke the eerie silence. As I descended, I counted each step and by the time I reached bottom, I had counted one hundred and thirty steps from street level to the base of the catacombs.

I stopped to read the historical plaque at the entrance to the catacombs. It explained that the catacombs had begun as large limestone quarries on the outskirts of the city. The light-coloured limestone was extracted and used in the construction of many of Paris's buildings, including the cathedral of Notre-Dame. Many of these mines were uncharted and eventually forgotten. In 1774 there was a series of road cave-ins. Human bones were unearthed from cemeteries adjacent to the cave-ins, in particular the Cemetery of Les Innocents. There had also been an overpopulation of bodies in many of the city's cemeteries, which gave rise to improper burials, open graves and unearthed corpses. The stench had become intolerable, and with people living in the proximity, fears of a deadly epidemic forced the authorities into action.

After a commission was named to investigate the state of the Parisian underground, the decision was made to move the remains of more than six million people into subterranean passageways being renovated to reinforce the streets above. In the early nineteenth century, the catacombs were transformed from a disorganized bone repository into a visitable mausoleum filled with carefully arranged human bones.

As if to give me warning, *"Arrête! C'est ici l'empire de la Mort* ("Stop! This is the Empire of the Dead") was written above the ossuary entrance. I entered a narrow tunnel where the faint smell of dampness filled the air. Shallow troughs carved into the floor along the base of the walls carried a trickle of water. Skulls and femurs, stacked floor-to-ceiling, lined the halls and caverns along each side. Marble plaques identified cemeteries that had relinquished bones and rusty gates blocked passages leading to the further reaches of the catacombs not open to the public.

I entered a circular room with an immense central pillar constructed from stacked human bones, and as I stood there, surrounded by the bones of countless people, I realized my family had something in common with them. We too were forced to move from our home, and like these remains, we had arrived at a place we did not belong. It made me wonder again where Farah came from. I was an immigrant and I was certain she was one, too. It wasn't just the slight accent I detected, but her overall philosophy of life that convinced me that she, like me, was an outsider.

But when I asked her she had replied, "I'm a *Canadian*."

Looking at all the misplaced bones surrounding me brought a great flash of inspiration—an image of three people, isolated within a crowd, and no matter how hard they try to make themselves visible, the crowd pays no attention and ignores them. I knew the trauma of being marginalized and of not feeling part of society. I was certain that if Farah ever saw the image I had in mind she would understand the intended message. It would represent the perfect metaphor for the isolation I'm sure she felt as all immigrants feel.

I touched the kerchief inside my jacket pocket.

"Farah, though you are one of the three marginalized people represented in the image, I want you to know that not everyone in your new home thinks of you as invisible," I said to myself.

I had found my inspiration for a new project.

That evening, as I lay in bed, images of crowds materialized in my mind's eye, people of all shape and sizes, women and men, young and old. As I imagined this parade of people, I fell into a deep sleep. A frightening dream assailed me. I was back in the catacombs and I could hear Farah calling for help from beyond the gates of the forbidden tunnels. I tried to crash the gates but no matter how hard I pushed they remained shut. I could hear the panic in Farah's voice as she called for help. Terrified, I ran along the main tunnel in the hope I would encounter someone who could help.

"Help, help, please someone help!" I hollered.

All I got back was an eerie silence.

Twenty-Three

THE FOLLOWING MORNING I AWOKE ANXIOUS FOR THE day to start. I opened the window and peered down at the sun-drenched streets. Immediately following breakfast, I gathered my sketchbook and pencil. I checked my camera to make sure the battery was fully charged and then left my studio in search of a crowd.

I started along Quai de l'Hôtel de Ville and then made a right turn onto Pont Marie. Halfway across the bridge, I heard an accordion pumping out a popular Parisian song. I stopped and looked over the railing and watched a boat loaded with people leisurely moving along the Seine. Some sang in tune with the accordion, with their wine glasses raised, others danced on the deck, drinking wine and laughing. Along the shores of the river, several groups sat on lawn chairs, people reading or talking and sipping wine from long stem glasses.

I wondered what these folks were doing drinking wine in the morning—in the open and in front of everyone—and then chuckled to myself. I was in Paris, not Toronto, and as I gazed upon the banks of the Seine and listened to the trees rustling in the wind, I felt a pain in my heart and longed for Farah's presence. I wished I could reach out and take her hand in mine.

Placing the sketchbook on the wide stone banister of the bridge, I made a quick drawing of the scene and wrote a note next to it.

My dearest Farah,
I pray all is fine with you and that you have not forgotten me. I am on Pont Marie, the bridge that crosses the Seine, in the vicinity of my studio. The view is beautiful. I wish you were here. I did a little drawing for you and wrote a little poem to go along with it. I hope you like it and it will give you a feeling for this beautiful place.
Much love,
Vittorio

P.S. I miss you terribly.

ON PONT MARIE

As I walk on Pont Marie
Across La Seine
Spanning the left and right bank
Connecting two countries
A king and a queen

Its stone barriers
Marked with the name of a noble lady
Marie de Medici Queen of France
Noble she was
But not nearly as noble as you

In the horizon
Along the river
Notre-Dame looks at me
As if with pity

I walk alone
In search of where you are
In all the ladies that pass me by
I look for a face that might be you

It is my wish
To have you at my side
And walk with me
Across this bridge

I dream of kissing you at Notre-Dame
And to place our lock
On the Bridge of Love
Our love sealed forever more.

On the other side of Pont Marie, Notre Dame overflowed with visitors. Here was a crowd like I had envisioned. I stood on my toes, holding my camera tight, then knelt on the square flagstones and shot from different angles to better the chance of getting something that would prove useful for the crowd painting I had planned.

At the Musée d'Orsay, a museum housed in a former historic train station featuring nineteenth-century French Art, I rode the elevator to the top floor and took pictures of the crowds in the main hall, of people pointing their fingers at works of art and of people concentrating intently on something far off at the end of the main hall. I searched for people of many different shapes and sizes, men and women, middle-aged, young and old, and of various ethnicities. Cour Napoléon, the courtyard of Louvre, provided me with everything I could wish for in a crowd. I took as many shots as I could without being a public nuisance.

On my way to the Centre Georges Pompidou, I stopped at a cafe on Rue Vieille du Temple for a rest and coffee. A young couple at an adjacent table hugged and kissed in plain sight for everyone to see. I wished Farah and I had that. I finished my espresso and continued on my quest. A poster on a wall caught my eye. It advertised the opening of an exhibition of paintings by an artist named Lahey Cantor at the Gallery Vieille du Temple that very evening. I wrote down the address in my sketchbook and moved on.

Before reaching the centre, I had a sudden change of mind and decided I had taken enough pictures to start the drawing process. I made my way to a print shop along narrow streets and got the pictures I had taken printed.

Back in the studio, I drew a dozen faces on a large piece of paper with all of them looking forward toward the right side edge of the paper. I made a conscious effort to select a variety of physical types so the crowd would represent people of different ages and backgrounds. I worked furiously and composed different group combinations. I gave no indication of the spectacle the crowd was looking at.

Within the crowd, I included three marginalized individuals. A man waving his hand would represent me as an immigrant, forever caught between two worlds, never knowing where he belonged. Though surrounded by a crowd, he would radiate a feeling of loss and isolation. It was important to me for the viewer to feel empathy for his plight, to be aware of how it felt to be rejected and always relegated to the outside.

Next, I drew Farah. I began sketching her from the recesses of my heart what I saw and how I felt when I was with her. She would represent potential fulfillment and acceptance. I moved my pencil over the paper in an attempt to draw her likeness, not so much with my hand, but with my heart. I had no desire to make a well-crafted drawing to please the eye. Line and composition and other fine details were nothing to me if the drawing missed Farah's character, expression and soul.

I worked furiously, trying to draw her face as I envisioned it in my heart, an intimate impression of her deep brown eyes, the shape of her lips, the curves of her cheekbones. But I failed.

When I glanced at my watch I saw that it was eight in the evening. I had been so engrossed in my new project that I hadn't noticed the time passing. The exhibition opening was in an hour. I changed into dress clothes and started for the Gallery Vieille du Temple.

Twenty-Four

I WALKED ALONG THE RUE VIEILLE DU TEMPLE—ONE OF the most charming districts in Paris—and saw the cafés crowded with people and couples leisurely strolling about the sidewalk talking and laughing. Boutiques, brasseries and French restaurants sat on every corner. The weekends, I discovered, were reserved for pedestrians only and really brought the street alive. People stood talking and drinking wine on the sidewalk in front of the art gallery. Inside a woman walked among the visitors offering red and white wine. I accepted a glass of red and sipped it as I viewed the artist's work. Visitors were busy around me discussing things in French. I wished I knew the language so I could take part in the conversations but all I could do was listen and observe.

The back of a woman across the room caught my eye.

"It couldn't be," I whispered to myself as wine ran down the corners of my mouth.

Yet those curves, the dark wavy hair, the short stature...

"Farah!" I called out without thinking.

There was no response except for a few people nearby who looked at me. The woman finally turned and for a split second I caught a glimpse of her face. My heart quickened—she was Farah's spitting image. Was it possible she had decided to come to Paris and surprise me at this art opening? I found myself in the middle of the room unable to resist her pull. As I drew near her, I determined she was not Farah. The woman wore a black skirt that fell to slightly above her knees, and the low cut of her white blouse exposed part of her breast and shining collarbone. Smooth skin covered high cheekbones and framed a set of sparkling dark eyes. The brilliant red of her lips made them lush and inviting. She was definitely a beautiful creature.

I wished to speak with her but decided I should walk around the gallery to gather my nerves and take a better look at the artwork so that I would have something meaningful to say when I spoke to her later in the evening. The paintings didn't hold my attention for long. I had seen the work of an artist in Canada with a similar style.

I watched people approach Farah's double and congratulate her. So, she was the artist whose work was on exhibit. I made my way a little closer to her and wondered if she spoke English. I heard her say "Thank you very much" and knew she did. I walked up to her with my nerves tight as a string on a bow.

"Hello, Miss Cantor," I said and extended my hand. "My name is Vittorio Lampi. I'm here in Paris for the summer doing research for my new artwork."

"It's a pleasure to meet you," she said. "Please call me Lahey."

"I like your work," I said. "I see in it both a reference to a personal history and a method of working that very much mirrors the present. It gives the work a life of its own."

"Thank you very much," she responded with a friendly smile.

"Are you a permanent resident of Paris?" I asked.

She was about to answer when a man took her attention away from our conversation. But before moving on she glanced back at me and said, "Please stay until after the opening. We could go for a glass of wine later if you like."

Her smile was both mesmerizing and inviting.

"I would love to," I said. "It's nice of you to ask."

Later after the opening celebration ended, Lahey and I sat on bright yellow chairs at deep red tables on the patio at Le Moderne Café on Rue Sanit-Antoine drinking wine. It was just a short walk from my studio,

"Do you live in Paris?" I asked her.

"I've been here almost a year but I'm returning home soon."

"Where do you come from?"

"Israel. More precisely, Haifa."

"I've never been there but would love to visit someday."

"I think you would love it there. Let me know when you do. You can stay at my place for a short while."

"You are very kind. Thanks for the offer. I may take you up on it someday."

"All you have to do is find your way there."

Lahey smiled as we talked and paid close attention to what I said. I had the feeling she found me attractive. Although it was mixed with guilt, I also felt a physical attraction to her, and this young woman, a replica of Farah, stole me away from the inner turmoil that rarely left me. When it came time to leave, I did not protest when she suggested we walk to my studio so she could see my work.

I was happy I had kept the place tidy aside from some clothes draped over the chair, which I tossed in the entrance closet. I found two clean tumblers and poured us some brandy. We stood in the middle of my studio with drinks in hand and looked at the drawing of the crowd I had worked on earlier in the day.

She gently reached for my hand and softly said, "Your drawing, though not finished, is very moving."

"Thank you for saying so," I said.

As I explained the concept of the drawing to her, I felt her fingers glide on top of mine. I stopped speaking. My gaze fell on our hands where mine burned beneath hers. My heart beat fast. The air between us felt electrified. We were kissing before I could draw my next breath. She gently pushed me away and began undressing, her movements slow and deliberate. I watched every article of clothing slip silently to the floor. She stepped over her scattered garments, displaying her nakedness in the glow of the floor lamp.

My body trembled with fear and desire and guilt.

"Come," she said.

I wondered if a naked Farah would look like this beautiful woman standing in front of me. I went to Lahey. We kissed with passion. I unzipped my trousers. She placed a hand inside my pants.

I failed to come alive. My heart was elsewhere.

"What's wrong, Vittorio?" she whispered.

"I'm sorry," I said. "It's not you. It's me. You're one of the most desirable and beautiful women I've ever seen...but I can't do this."

"What's the matter?" she said and took a step back.

"There's someone else in my heart."

Her pout turned into a slight smile.

"Well, she's a lucky woman to have such loyalty."

We stood quietly, not knowing what to do next. Then an idea struck me.

"May I make a drawing of you?" I asked.

She eyed me with suspicion.

"What for?"

"For the drawing of the crowd painting we just looked at on the wall."

"Hmm." She gave a thoughtful look. "How would you like me to pose?"

I glanced around.

"You sit on the chair and I'll draw your face so I can place it at the bottom right side of the drawing," I said.

She agreed and so I covered her with a blanket and set to work.

"If you don't mind, I'd like to have a three-quarter view of your face," I said.

She angled herself as I instructed. I began to draw her face directly onto the big paper on the wall. She stared at me silently as I worked. After a while, Lahey's face peered out from the corner of the paper with an intensity that engaged the viewer as being complicit with the mood and action of the crowd.

I stood back and examined my work.

"Can I have a look?" she said.

"By all means."

She stood up, walked over to the wall, and studied my work.

"That's truly good," she said. "Thank you."

"No!" I said. "I thank you."

I was thanking her for not only modelling for me, but also for bringing a bit of Farah to Paris.

Twenty-Five

I WOKE VERY EARLY THE NEXT MORNING AND COULDN'T
get back to sleep. I lay in bed and looked at the archipelago of old
stains covering the ceiling. Leonardo da Vinci claimed he could
see figures in stains. I thought if I looked hard enough, I might
have the same experience. Perhaps Farah's face would appear.

My mind was so clouded with thoughts of Farah that it made
it impossible to allow room for anything else. I stubbornly held
on to the belief that no one should be deprived of true love without the very best of reasons. The fact that Farah was married
would certainly be reason enough for most people, but love was
confounding, not logical. It truly made no sense that an older
man would fall in love with a much younger, not to mention
married, woman. But I still couldn't bring myself to believe that
all was lost before it even started. Farah had managed to inexplic-
ably fill the emptiness in my life.

I imagined her lying at my side, her eyes glued to mine, in
that deep penetrating stare she had captured within me. I carried
her in my mind the same way I carried my heart in my chest.

I could never forget the tenderness in her voice and in her
subtle movements. Like a secret code with no words of explana-
tion, all those special gestures spoke silently to me. They said, "I
need you."

I missed her beautiful laughter and the way the two of us enjoyed sharing little things that few people took the time to consider. Not being able to mail her a letter or contact her made me unsure of the difference between the real Farah and the Farah I dreamed of holding my hand as my wife. In my dreams I could see her in my studio, the aroma of her body permeating the air. I could see us lying awake in each other's arms, completely alone, in our private world, inseparable.

A sudden and loud chattering cut my daydreaming. I rose and peered out my open window. The grey dreariness of the early morning had made way for a clear blue sky and the warm rays of the Mediterranean sun. Two men were having an animated discussion in front of the café across the street.

I looked back at the crowd drawing that hung on the wall. It was lit by the wash of morning light coming through the window. The drawing had the drama I wanted, but I wondered if through more research and hard work it could be even better. The addition of Lahey's face had made a significant difference. The look in her eyes, which directly challenged the viewer, created a moment of tension and heightened the viewing experience. I tried not to think about what took place when Lahey visited my studio. The embarrassment was still palpable.

I reached for my sketchbook and stood by the window. I started drawing a scene of Notre-Dame's spires peeking through the trees on the shores of the Seine. I concentrated heavily on the drawing and the hours seemed to vanish. When I lifted the pencil from the paper and studied the drawing for a moment, a knock on the door stole my attention. When I opened it, I was stunned to see Lahey. I stood in the doorway with my mouth agape.

"Hello, Vittorio," she said, noticing my look of surprise and grinning wildly. "How have you been?"

I could feel my cheeks warm as I pictured her naked again.

"What a surprise to see you," I said.

"Don't let that moment bother you," she said. "I admire you for being true to the person you love. Besides, there's no reason why we can't spend time together as artists."

"That's true," I said with relief.

"I'm going back to Israel in a couple of days and was wondering if you wanted to visit the Musée National du Moyen Âge with me."

"Sure," I said. "But now that I have found a friend to enjoy Paris with, I'm sorry to hear you're leaving."

"Well, I am not quite ready to leave, but leave I must," she said. "You need not worry, though. You'll make more friends as time goes by. What if we leave for the museum now so we can beat the crowds?"

"I'll grab my keys and lock up."

Lahey may not have been Farah, but she reminded me of her, and now I had a friend to enjoy the day with. Paris didn't seem so lonely in that moment.

Upon entering the Musée National du Moyen Âge I didn't feel as overwhelmed as I had when I first entered the Louvre. But it was magnificent. The architectural beauty of the museum was awe-inspiring. The first area we visited was the Notre-Dame gallery. Sunlight poured through the glass ceiling.

"Two of the walls were originally part of an ancient Roman bath," Lahey said and laughed. "Can you visualize this room filled with naked Romans?"

"That would be quite the sight," I responded.

Her giggle made me chuckle.

"There are an awful lot of stone heads displayed in this room," I said.

Lahey's face lit up.

"Those heads once belonged on top of columns that lined the entrance portal of Notre-Dame Cathedral," she said.

"How did they end up here?"

"During the French Revolution, the Paris citizens bashed the heads off the statues. The fact the statues represented the Kings of Judah didn't help matters," she said and raised an eyebrow.

We walked through the museum browsing an amazing collection of sculptures, reliquaries, paintings, books, ivories, furniture, heraldry, glass and metalwork.

"This is certainly an authentic medieval experience," I said with a huge grin.

"If you think this is great wait until you see the tapestry of *The Lady and the Unicorn*."

"I can hardly wait," I said and followed Lahey up the stairs to the top floor, where the tapestries were presented in a darkened room and arranged in a circle that made for intimate viewing. We stood just inside the entrance and adjusted our eyes to the dim light. A small group of people gathered around the tapestries discussing the imagery in the woven works before them.

I was struck by the enchanting combination of a deep red ground strewn with a rich variety of flora—pine, orange sessile, oak, holly trees—and the repetition of a coat of arms motif with three white crescents on a blue background. The animals on display—including rabbits, monkeys and birds—also caught my attention. But above all, what made the greatest impact was the palpable relationship I saw between the Lady and her Unicorn.

"Who is the Lady?" I heard a person ask a guide when we got closer to the group of visitors.

"Jean Le Viste, a lawyer and counsellor to the court of King Louis XI, commissioned the cycle of tapestries," the guide replied.

"As far as the Lady in the tapestry is concerned, it's thought she may have been Jean Le Viste's own wife, but no one knows for certain. However, she definitely looks like a noblewoman."

The Lady held me spellbound. I finally tore my gaze away and looked at the Unicorn. I could almost taste the longing on the beast's face and feel the despair in his eyes as he looked upon the Lady whom he could never have. A cold shiver ran through me. *The Lady and the Unicorn* tapestry touched me in a way that was very immediate and personal. I became overemotional and wanted to leave. I would return another day on my own. I turned away and looked at Lahey.

"Would you like a cup of coffee?"

"By all means," she said. "Are you okay?"

"I'm not sure," I said.

"You look like you've seen a ghost, Vittorio"

"I'll be fine. I just need some fresh air."

We made our way back down the museum stairs in silence and walked to a patio café.

"Better now?" Lahey asked as we sipped espressos.

"I still feel a bit strange," I said.

I didn't say anything more on the subject and she didn't press the matter further.

"We must keep in touch," Lahey said and pulled out a pen and piece of paper from her purse. She wrote something down and passed it to me.

"My address and phone number," she said and flashed her beautiful smile. "Send me a postcard. I love getting postcards."

Twenty-Six

I RETURNED TO MY STUDIO APARTMENT STILL SHIV-
ering from the cold chill that settled upon me in front of *The
Lady and the Unicorn* tapestries. It wasn't the first time a great
work of art had moved me to such heightened emotions. Yet
there was something different this time. My mind roamed all
over my mental map until I resolved to go back to the museum
the moment it opened the next morning.

I poured some brandy in a tumbler and stood at the window.
I sipped it slowly hoping it might clear my head. Darkness was
descending on Paris. The steeples of Notre-Dame and the dome
of the Pantheon appeared to have a soft and mysterious glow. I
wondered what Farah would think of *The Lady and the Unicorn*
tapestries. She had become the gauge by which I measured
everything of importance in my life, the filter through which I
screened my every thought and desire.

I finished the brandy and, feeling overwhelmed, lay down
in bed for a moment. When I woke up it was light. I got up
and washed and dressed. I checked my coat pocket to make sure
Farah's kerchief was still there, and was out the door and at the
museum by nine thirty. A few visitors already waited by the entrance. I purchased the admission ticket and ran up the stairs to
the tapestry room before anyone else. I walked by each of the

six tapestries slowly to get an overall feeling for the theme each represented and then returned to the beginning.

In the first tapestry, "Taste," the Lady stands at the centre of the composition. She reaches into a dish of sweets held by a maidservant. The Unicorn and a lion stand on their hind legs on either side of her. A parakeet, monkey and dog can also be seen. Numerous flowers and fauna float over a deep red background. I was reminded of the Garden of Eden, where love, pleasure and virtue flourished, unburdened by the pressures of life. The tapestry clearly depicts the beginning of a love story.

In the second tapestry, "Hearing," the Lady plays a small pipe organ and the Unicorn and lion, again framing the Lady, listen intently. Listening was certainly the subject but I also thought pleasure was a theme. I once saw the beautiful joy on Farah's face when we sat in the car in comfortable silence listening to music. I wondered if the Lady was encouraging the viewer to strive for a higher and a greater spiritual intellect represented in the music.

I moved on to the next tapestry, "Sight." The Lady hosts the Unicorn partly on her lap and holds a mirror up to him. The Unicorn looks at his own reflection and sees only desire and longing in his heart. The Lady looks away as if she has no need to look at the Unicorn's reflection because she can see him in her mind's eye. While the Unicorn has been invited into her garden of pleasure, it seems the Lady's refusal to look at the Unicorn's reflection denies him the pleasures of her garden. He cannot partake.

A new chill, stronger than the one I had felt the previous night, crept up my spine.

In the fourth tapestry, "Smell," the Lady, again framed by the unicorn and the lion, fashions a wreath of flowers as a maidservant holds a basket. Beside them, a monkey sniffs a stolen flower.

"Why smell?" I asked myself out loud.

Then I remembered the emotions I had felt when I first lifted Farah's kerchief to my nose. The scent connected me to her. Each time I brought a rose to Farah, she had smelled it over and over again. I could tell by her expression that it had heightened her sensorial desire, the way love can.

My curiosity reached a feverish pitch. I thought there might be a connection between the Lady and Farah that I needed to explore. The mystery the tapestries presented drove me to hunger for answers, the way Farah's mystery drove me to such distraction that I would forget even to eat.

In the next tapestry, "Touch," the Lady reaches for the Unicorn's horn. It isn't clear if the Lady is in the middle of removing her hand from the horn or if she wants to grasp it. Is she welcoming the Unicorn or withdrawing from him? Is the Unicorn's presence welcomed or rejected? It appears the Unicorn wants to be with her. He gazes at the Lady with an expression of love. His longing for her is palpable. The Unicorn was a recognizable figure. I knew this character.

I stood in front of the final tapestry, "*À Mon Seul Désir*," and felt like I was standing on a surface charged with electrical currents. "*À Mon Seul Désir*" is written across the top of a tent the Lady stands in front of. I didn't know what the words meant. I looked about the room to see if there was someone who could translate them for me. I walked over to a guide speaking to a small group of people in English. When the opportunity presented itself, I moved forward and said, "Excuse me, sir, but would you be so kind as to translate the phrase written at the top of the tent for me?"

I pointed to the tapestry.

"It can be translated as "My One Sole Desire," the man said in a thick English accent.

"Thank you, sir. You are very kind."

"My pleasure," the man said and turned back to his tour group.

"My One Sole Desire," I said quietly to myself.

I walked back to the tapestry and stared at it again. The Lady has a smile on her face, as if she knows something only she is privy to. Her maidservant stands to her right holding an open chest. The Lady looks to be placing the necklace she wore in the other tapestries into the chest. This is the only tapestry in which the Lady is seen smiling. Who was this Lady? What was she hiding behind that smile? I saw the same ambiguity in "My One Sole Desire" as I had in the other five tapestries. On one hand, the Lady appears to be putting the necklace into the chest, but on a second look, she could be lifting it out of the chest. If she is taking the necklace out of the chest, it could mean that she accepts the pleasures of the five senses represented in the other tapestries and along with it the love of the Unicorn. On the other hand, if she is placing the necklace into the chest, she could be denying the passion aroused by the five senses.

I couldn't take my eyes off the Lady and heard myself ask, "Who are you?"

The answer came to me as soon as the question escaped my lips. "Farah."

Although she hadn't come to Paris in the flesh, Farah had been here all along.

I thought about what she had said about love before I left for Paris. In setting aside the necklace, the Lady depicted in the tapestries is saying the same thing.

"Can you?" Farah asked after telling me that chaste love was the only kind of love she was interested in with me.

I was not able to answer her question at the time.

I felt the same longing so evident in the way the Unicorn looked at the Lady, and like the Unicorn, I tried hard to prove I was worthy of her love. In my attempt to win Farah's love, I sometimes felt like I was alone on a boat out in the middle of a lake on a clear night, endlessly trying to scoop the reflection of the moon from the water's surface. Like the Unicorn, I was brave and honourable. I did whatever Farah asked me to do. I willingly subjected myself to numerous tests in order to earn her trust and love. When I displeased her I felt like I had been cast into a pit devoid of light without any possibility of redemption.

I was Farah's Unicorn.

A great desire came over me to touch the Lady. I wanted to be united with Farah in body and spirit. I looked around to make sure the guard was not watching and placed a hand on the tapestry. A profound sadness filled my heart. Could I ever accept a love that sought nothing but the yearning emotions of being in love? I sat down on a bench by the tapestry, reached for my pen and sketchbook and started writing Farah a note:

> My most dear and sweet Farah,
> I am sitting by a tapestry called the Lady and
> the Unicorn. I am so taken by what I see that
> I must attempt to write a poem about the
> experience so you will know how I feel. I hope
> you will not just visualize the beauty of the
> tapestry when you read it, but also recognize
> the thoughts I have of you in my heart, which I
> hope the words express, however inadequate.
>
> Yours always,
> Vittorio

THE BEDAZZLED UNICORN

I am the Unicorn lost in the wonder that is you
And in the presence of your beauty
I delight in my torment
I drown in the splendour of your eyes
And like the bedazzled Unicorn
I no longer recognize what I am
Part human, part beast
For love and for you, my dear Lady
I have happily died
You have enslaved my heart
Which I can no longer retrieve
And your prisoner of love
I shall forever be.

Twenty-Seven

I HAD A DREAM OF FARAH SO VIVID THAT WHEN I WOKE up—or I thought I had woken up—the room seemed filled with her presence. I glanced across the darkness to see if she really was there. Everything seemed different, airy and expansive, as if the room had no walls to maintain its shape. In my semiconscious state I could hear the sound of a piano and singing and Farah's laughter. Glasses tinkled, doors creaked open and heavy footsteps thudded. A louder, piercing sound fully woke me up.

I got out of bed in a groggy stupor and shuffled to the window. I listened more closely and determined it was the knell of church bells ringing from every corner of the city. The call to attend Sunday morning church was evident.

Below my window, people dressed in their Sunday best walked with purpose. Many women wore scarves on their heads as they crossed the bridge leading to Notre-Dame. The Seine was quiet. No boat rode its currents this morning.

I was so focused on the early morning bustle I had nearly forgotten last night's dream, and then the image of the Lady and the Unicorn dissolved my view of the world in front of me. The vision was so vivid that I could not resist the desire to share it with Farah.

My dearest and most loved Farah,

Given the wall of silence we agreed to maintain, I can only trust that all is well with you. I hope you think of me. I think of you not only consciously during the day but also unconsciously at night in my sleep. Last night was no exception. I dreamt the Lady in the tapestry came to visit me while I was standing in the golden reception room at the Musée d'Orsay.

In my dream, the shapes of the ceiling lights reflected in the mirrors caught my attention and as I gazed at the reflections, the Lady from the tapestry suddenly appeared in their haziness. I wondered what she was doing at the Musée d'Orsay. As she came closer to where I stood, the Lady's hair, with loose waves cascading over her shoulders, changed from blonde to black, and her face changed to yours.

Seeing you standing in front of me made me speechless. My insides smouldered with excitement. Our eyes met in the same way they met the first time I saw you. I was about to say something when you lifted your hand and stopped me. "Come," you said with a smile. I extended my hand to yours to hold, but then your glow promptly evaporated into the lights.

Please forgive my silly dream. Miss You.

Always I remain yours in love,
Vittorio

I finished writing my note to Farah around midmorning and decided to look through some drawings of the Paris catacombs I had done from memory after visiting them. It came to me as I stared at them that in comparison to North America, where death is kept at bay or hidden as much as possible, in other parts of the world death was out in the open and often celebrated. Mexicans celebrated the Day of the Dead which, according to folklore, the Aztecs began some three thousand years ago—we should not grieve the loss of beloved ancestors who passed but should instead celebrate their lives and once a year welcome the return of their spirits to the land of the living. On the Day of the Dead they place thousands of chrysanthemums, designed in many forms, over tombstones and graves.

As I mulled over these ideas, they inspired me to do a drawing with many different types of chrysanthemums scattered among the bones I had seen in the Paris catacombs.

I turned on the radio so I could listen to music while I worked. One of my favourite pieces, Mozart's "Requiem," was playing and it put me in a good mood. I took a large piece of paper and drew the flowers from different angles and in different sizes to give the drawing the depth I wanted. I drew each flower, starting from its centre and working my way out, by outlining hundreds of petals, one by one, until dozens of flowers filled the composition. At the top of the paper, above the bones and flowers, I drew a burning fire with the flames reaching to the top.

I was so engrossed in the drawing that I had forgotten about lunch and only realized the extent of my hunger when my stomach growled. I stopped and gazed at what I had done. It was a visual requiem.

"Farah would be proud of you, Vittorio," I said to myself.

Twenty-Eight

A NIGHT OF HEAVY RAIN AND ITS PERSISTENT POUNDING against the windows kept me from a sound sleep. I tossed and turned and then finally switched on the light. Postcards from Dennis and Paul lay on the nightstand. They reminded me that I would be returning home to Toronto in three weeks. I got out of bed and poured myself a glass of wine. I stepped over to the window. Darkness and fog obscured Pont Marie. The streets were quiet with only the casual car passing by. As I stood at the window, eager for the light of dawn to arrive, my thoughts turned to Farah. I drank the wine slowly, hoping it would make me drowsy, and walked over to the calendar on the wall. I took out my pen and started marking down the days until I would see her again.

I wondered if Farah longed for me to return. I had longed for her during my entire time in Paris, mad with desire for her, one moment feeling extremely happy and the next feeling utter despair. I had waited my whole life for her and was now haunted by her endless refusals. Had I fallen in love with a woman who didn't truly exist?

Needing to clear my head, I decided to go for an early morning walk. I put on my coat and checked the mailbox on my way out. Lahey had sent a postcard. The cover showed a view of the north slope of Mount Carmel and Haifa's most iconic site, the immaculately landscaped terraces of the Bahá'í Gardens. I was touched that she still thought of me. On the back of the postcard she wrote:

> Hello Vittorio, how are you? As you can see,
> Haifa is beautiful.
> I'm working in my studio and doing okay.
> My offer still stands.
> Lahey

I pocketed the postcard and made my way to Pont Marie. I crossed the bridge and stopped at a twenty-four-hour depanneur. I scoured their postcards and came across one with a painting by Theodor Gericault. It had an image of a dead cat on top of a table with its head hanging over the edge. I had seen the original painting in the Louvre. The beauty of the paint application had greatly impressed me. It looked like it had been created in recent times. The more I thought about it, though, it was probably not the best image to send Lahey. I flipped through some more postcards and came upon another work by Gericault, a drawing depicting three cats in playful poses. On the back I wrote:

> Hello, Lahey
> Thank you for thinking of me. I'm doing fine.
> Getting ready to return to Canada. My visit to
> your studio will have to wait. Thank you for
> the invite.
> All the best,
> Vittorio

Twenty-Nine

ON MY LAST DAY IN PARIS I DECIDED TO VISIT THE Centre Pompidou to see the work of Palestinian artist Mona Hatoum. André, my next door neighbour, had told me it was a terrific show. I entered the front doors of the exhibition area and was welcomed by a billboard with the unsettling image of Mona Hatoum herself in a work called *Over My Dead Body.* In the picture, she is shown in silhouette with a model soldier holding a rifle aimed between her eyes, poised on the ridge of her nose. I read this work as a comment on gender roles and a reminder to the viewer that conventional wars were still going on in many parts of the world. Hatoum's ideas were not unlike my own. Her work was charged with social and political overtones, which were greatly expressed in works such as *Hot Spot,* a large wire-framed globe, with continents outlined in red neon, which I think is meant to convey the whole planet is moving towards a fiery end if we are not careful in how we treat it.

It was late afternoon when I left Centre Pompidou. Given this would be my last evening in Paris and that I had been careful with my summer spending, I decided to splurge and treat myself to a nice dinner. Although I knew it was going to be expensive, I elected to dine at Les Deux Magots, located in a touristy area, but beautiful and alive with people. I got a seat at the front of the bistro with a great view of people coming and going. The place had a great history, with a reputation of having hosted legendary writers and artists like Hemingway and Picasso. It took me back to the golden age of literature and Art Deco that I knew.

A waiter arrived arrayed in black and white in a bowtie. I ordered the beef and marrow stew, escargot, a glass of red wine and a bottle of mineral water.

After dinner I lingered, enjoying the sights and feeling that if I were to close my eyes, one of those great artists might come by and have a glass of wine with me and a lively conversation about art and literature. How wonderful it would be, I thought, to have Farah here with me on last day in Paris.

It was almost midnight when I finally looked at my watch. I paid my bill and strolled back to my studio, taking in every sight and sound one last time along the way. I topped off my final evening in Paris when I reached the studio with a last good shot of brandy. I stretched out on the bed with my back propped against the wall and thought about what Farah might say upon seeing me again. The combination of wine and brandy had the desired effect. I fell asleep.

Thirty

THE FAMILIAR SEEMED STRANGE WHEN THE PLANE landed in Toronto following my four-month sojourn to Paris. Busy wide roads replaced quaint cobblestone streets. No clay tile rooftops were to be seen. Already I missed the assortment of family-owned shops that specialized in a particular produce, cheese, bread, pastry and other delicious things. But Toronto was home, and Farah lived here.

The city was also home to my friends, Dennis and Paul. The day following my arrival I got in touch with Dennis.

"How's it going, you old goat?" I said over the phone.

"Hello, Vittorio, nice to have you back, but tone down your compliments. You haven't changed."

"You missed me even though you won't say so."

"Your head is big enough as it is."

"How is Paul? Can we get together this evening?"

"I'll give him a buzz. I'm sure he'd love to. See you soon."

"I'll have a glass of wine ready for you guys."

"That's more like it!"

Dennis and Paul arrived at my studio around nine o'clock each with a bottle of wine in hand.

"Hello, hello, hello!" I said and gave both a big hug. "Nice to see you boys. By the look of things, I guess you plan on doing a bit of drinking."

"We couldn't trust you to have enough wine on hand so we brought a couple of bottles along," Paul said with a chuckle.

I poured three glasses of wine. "I want to thank you guys for looking after things while I was away," I said. "To show you my appreciation I brought souvenirs."

"Hey, Paul," Dennis said winking at him. "Vittorio is trying to prove he is a nice guy. Can you believe it?"

"Nothing he does surprises me," Paul said as he raised his glass to Dennis.

I reached for the book on photography by Wolfgang Tillmans, considered a photographic innovator, and handed it to Dennis. He broke out in a smile when he took the book in his hands.

"This is fantastic. Thanks."

"I went specifically to Shakespeare and Company, on the West Bank in Paris, to get this book," I said. "Because you did such a great job finding someone to rent my studio for the summer, I also bought this for you at the Paris Opera House." I handed Dennis *Hymme la Môme*, a double CD by Edith Piaf.

"Oh, God, that's really terrific," he said and hugged me. "Thanks so much."

"Hey! What about me?" Paul said with a smirk on his face.

"Hold your horses!"

I handed Paul a book by Christopher Hitchens called *Arguably: Essays on Many Subjects*.

"Thanks a lot, Vittorio," Paul said. "This should make for some interesting reading."

"So, how did you make out in Paris?" Dennis asked.

"Paris was great though there were times I missed being with you two."

"Since we're talking about missing someone, how's it going with Farah?" Paul asked.

I let out a heavy sigh and placed my glass of wine on the table. "I haven't spoken to her since I left Toronto," I said.

"Holy shit!" Paul said. "Why the hell not?"

"We agreed to no contact while I was away."

"Jesus, Vittorio, that sounds strange to me," Dennis said.

"Well, I can tell you I'm very anxious to see her," I said. "But let's have another glass of wine and not get into it for now."

We stayed up until the early hours of the morning talking and drinking. We were like brothers again. I hadn't felt close to anyone since I left for Paris. I missed the feeling.

September finally arrived and the school year began. I waited patiently for our day and hour to arrive, fearing what might transpire. At noon on the first Wednesday after returning from Paris I sat at Tim Hortons and waited for Farah. I assumed she was still taking classes, but I didn't know what to expect. What if we had nothing to talk about after so long apart? Would we sit across from each other, like two strangers, enveloped in awkward silence? What would she say to me? What would I say to her?

I had rehearsed this moment in my mind a thousand times, but now that the time was near, I couldn't remember the words I was to say. I was bursting with anticipation and excitement at seeing her. Yet I thought our meeting could also end in disappointment or without resolution. Farah had promised me nothing. Owed me nothing. If she said we should not see each other again, then she would part a free woman—but I would never again be a free man.

I could no longer live without the question being answered once and for all—would Farah choose me or not? I did not know what I would do if she firmly rejected me. She had said in the past she could not leave her husband. I had an image of him as a good provider and a dependable man. I was jealous of his place in her life. Although I did not wish him harm, it was painful for me to think about Farah sleeping with him every night while I remained on the outside looking in, a situation no different from the three isolated immigrants in my crowd drawing.

I had to admit that keeping our love a secret had made it exciting at times. We could be in the coffee shop surrounded by customers and express our feelings for each other without touching—with just a look or a smile.

I glanced down at the leather-bound sketchbook on the table. So many of the drawings and writings in my Paris sketchbook had been completed with Farah in mind that I decided I would present it to her as a gift. I opened it and flipped through the pages. There were many drawings, poems, letters and other writings. Many sentences were crossed out with thick black lines—my struggles. They were flawed but honest and full of the love I felt for her.

The last page was blank and I decided to write one more note and a poem to Farah. I wanted something that would capture her full attention. To make her grow into my words like a flower in a garden.

With a trembling hand I got out my pencil and wrote:

My dearest love,

Having been away from you for so long my
heart is full of things I want to share with you.
I have no idea where to start or what words to
use. I hope that in my absence you thought of
me from time to time. God only knows not a
day passed that I didn't think of you and send

you my love. You are my goddess, Farah, my one and only love.

You may not be aware that I'm back in Toronto as we have had no communication since I left for Paris. I am at a loss to express my joy at the prospect of seeing you again.

Since arriving in Toronto, I have thought of nothing else, and I have not closed my eyes for a moment. I fear if I do not see you soon I will die from fatigue and lack of sleep!

I am so grateful for having found you, but the fact that you are not solely mine breaks my heart every minute of every day. I pray that after seeing you again, you will say you love me, and that I will not become a mere footnote on a page in your life.

My heart is full of longing for you. My thoughts go out to you, my beloved Farah. I am filled with anxiety as I wait to learn what fate has in store for both of us. Living without you would be unbearable. When you are not present, my world is shrouded in darkness. To put into words all that I feel would require the voice of a Rumi. Sadly, nature has not bestowed on me such a gift for words.

All I can say is I loved you in the past, I love you today, I will continue to love you tomorrow and forever.

Your devoted servant in love,
Vittorio

A RAY OF HOPE
Without you
The City of Love
Was as dark
As the empty desert
Of my heart
Far too long we've been apart
But thoughts of seeing you again
Brings a tremor to my heart
And a ray of hope
That was almost lost
I long for the moment
You'll be in my arms
But sometimes I fear
You may turn me away
Leaving me to wonder what could have been?

Farah did not show up.

Thirty-One

FOR SEVERAL WEEKS I DROVE TO THE COFFEE SHOP ON
Wednesday at noon and waited for Farah with no success. I was
desperate to see her and began showing up every day. Then it oc-
curred to me that perhaps she no longer attended school. Maybe
she was working. I needed to change tactics.

I got up early one morning and drove to her house with the
idea of arriving before she left home for school or work. I parked
my car down the street from her house at seven thirty and waited.
I planned to watch her leave the house and follow her to her destination. Each passing moment felt like an eternity.

An hour later, I saw Farah leave her house and walk down
the steps to the driveway. My heart raced after not seeing her for
such a long time. I followed her to the Humber College campus.
I parked my car far enough away so she wouldn't notice it. I
wanted to approach her immediately but decided to wait until
after her class. I didn't want to make her late.

I waited in my car and struggled with my emotions. Would
the waiting and the loneliness soon come to an end? Would she
join me? Or would my worst fears come to pass and all I would
ever be allowed were furtive glances and stolen moments—and
could I be happy with just that?

I had no doubt that if Farah's answer was no, then I would
never try and love again. I immediately vanquished the thought

from my mind. To think of life without her was as frightening to me as the thought of losing my life in front of a firing squad. I didn't know what I would do if she refused to leave her husband.

Students walked in and out of the building. I kept a keen eye on the door and on Farah's car. I didn't want to miss her. I must have checked my watch a million times before I finally saw Farah exit the building. I managed to get out of my car without her seeing me and made my way to her car and stood beneath a nearby tree. She looked more mature as I watched her walk towards her vehicle—as if she had gone through some sort of change—and she was more beautiful than I even remembered. As she reached into her purse for her car keys, I stepped forward.

"Farah," I said.

She turned her head and spun around in my direction. Her lips parted, as if in shock, and then she gave me a small smile. She moved fast towards me. I could feel the knot in my stomach tighten. I wanted to run to her but my legs wouldn't move.

"Vittorio, is that really you?" she said when she reached me and threw her arms around me.

"Yes, Farah, it really is me."

Her embrace didn't last long. She quickly dropped her arms and took a step back.

"How are you?" I said. "You look more beautiful than ever."

The pink in her cheeks deepened.

"Thank you. You look good. How was Paris?"

I searched for the right words but didn't quite know how to say that Paris would have been wonderful had you been there with me but without you it was lonely.

"Fine," I finally said. "I missed you terribly."

She stayed silent.

"Let's talk in the car," I said.

We climbed inside and sat in awkward silence. I ached to take her in my arms and to passionately kiss her. She sat next to me, not moving, staring straight ahead as if she were in a dark movie theatre waiting for the next scene.

"Farah, in these past four months I've had a lot of time to think about what I would say to you when I saw you next," I said. "I waited all summer for the opportunity to tell you as definitively as I possibly can that—I love you with all my heart and I'm willing to do whatever it takes for us to be together."

She remained silent.

After another long moment the ringtone of her phone made us both jump. She ignored it, let out a deep breath, and turned her head to me. Her dark eyes, rimmed with tears, locked on mine with great intensity. The tension was almost unbearable.

"That's not possible," she said.

"What do you mean, *not possible?*"

"There can be no *us*," she said.

"I don't understand. What do you mean, no *us?*"

She bit her lower lip.

"I'm pregnant!"

"Pregnant?" I said with disbelief.

"Yes. Going on three months," she said.

I could feel the blood drain from my face. It should have been my baby she was carrying and not someone else's—not even her husband's!

I clenched my fist, ready to punch an invisible foe, and felt like a man trodden under the boots of fate.

Farah turned her head and stared straight through the windshield.

"Did you miss me at all?" I finally said breaking the silence that had enveloped us.

"I did," she said. "But does it really matter now?"

"It does," I said. "I still want you. I love you."

"Stop!" she cried out. "What you envision for us is nothing but an illusion. A dream! Nothing can possibly come of it. Please understand."

Farah's words felt like a blow to the chest. I couldn't breathe. I became dizzy. I lowered the window for some fresh air.

I heard the words I had dreaded most.

The Lady from the tapestry suddenly appeared before me. Now I knew the truth of her knowing smile and what she was doing with the necklace. I had no doubt. The Lady was placing the necklace *inside* the chest. It was renunciation after all.

I looked over at Farah. Tears trickled down her cheeks. She had banished me to the kingdom of the dead with no hope or promise of resurrection. There was no coming back from the underworld to be reunited with my beloved. I knew that. My eyes welled up. I handed her my Paris sketchbook.

"What is this?" she said.

"A gift to you from Paris," I said.

She hesitated for a moment and then took the sketchbook in her hands.

"You shouldn't have."

"I no longer need it."

Acknowledgements

I MUST START BY THANKING MY WIFE, DORIS, FOR HER patience during the time it took to write this novel and for supporting me throughout our fifty-year-plus marriage. I could not have done it without you, Doris.

Many thanks to Life Rattle Press and Laurie Kallis for the positive feedback and the support and energy put into the publishing of *Year of the Unicorn*. To my editor, John Dunford, endless gratitude for your support and invaluable input in making the book a better read.

A special thanks to my friend and former colleague, artist Robert Fones, for his generosity and boundless support. Thanks also to my former art student and promising author, David Kee, for lending me his sharp ear and for challenging me to do better. I also thank author Lisa Collicutt and Sarah Pereaux for their constructive input in the early stages of the novel.

www.ingramcontent.com/pod-product-compliance
Lightning Source LLC
Chambersburg PA
CBHW031957010726
47493CB00007B/2240